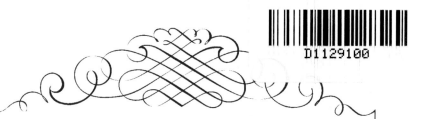

ISBN 978-1-334-22698-4
PIBN 10757391

1 MONTH OF
FREE
READING

at

www.ForgottenBooks.com

By purchasing this book you are eligible for one month membership to ForgottenBooks.com, giving you unlimited access to our entire collection of over 700,000 titles via our web site and mobile apps.

To claim your free month visit:

www.forgottenbooks.com/free757391

English
Français
Deutsche
Italiano
Español
Português

www.forgottenbooks.com

Mythology Photography **Fiction**
Fishing Christianity **Art** Cooking
Essays Buddhism Freemasonry
Medicine **Biology** Music **Ancient**
Egypt Evolution Carpentry Physics
Dance Geology **Mathematics** Fitness
Shakespeare **Folklore** Yoga Marketing
Confidence Immortality Biographies
Poetry **Psychology** Witchcraft
Electronics Chemistry History **Law**
Accounting **Philosophy** Anthropology
Alchemy Drama Quantum Mechanics
Atheism Sexual Health **Ancient History**
Entrepreneurship Languages Sport
Paleontology Needlework Islam
Metaphysics Investment Archaeology
Parenting Statistics Criminology
Motivational

IMPORTANT NOVELS

Aaron's Rod	By D. H. Lawrence
The Lost Girl	By D. H. Lawrence
Intrusion	By Beatrice Kean Seymour
Invisible Tides	mour
Escape	
The Widow's Cruse	By Hamilton Fyfe
The Fruit of the Tree	By Hamilton Fyfe

BATOUALA

BATOUALA

BY

RENÉ MARAN

NEW YORK
THOMAS SELTZER
1922

SJK

The Translation of This Book
Was Made by

ADELE SZOLD SELTZER

I Dedicate This Book
To My Dear Friend
MANOEL GAHISTO

PREFACE

Henri de Régnier, Jacques Boulenger, sponsors of this book, I should consider myself unfeeling were I not to use the very first lines of my preface to acknowledge all I owe to your kindness and advice.

You know how earnestly I wish for the success of this novel. To be sure, it is merely a series of etchings, but I have taken six years to complete it. I have taken six years to translate what I have heard and to describe what I have seen.

During those six years I did not yield once to the temptation to express my views. I have carried my scruples regarding objectivity so far as to suppress any reflections that others might attribute to me.

As a matter of fact the Negroes of

equatorial Africa are an unreflecting race. They have no critical faculties; and they never have had, nor ever will have, any intelligence. At least, so it is said. Wrongly, no doubt. For if unintelligence characterized the Negroes, there would be few Europeans in their country.

So my novel is altogether objective. It makes no attempt to explain: it states. It voices no indignation: it records. No other method would have been possible. Moonlight nights, as I sat reclining in my chaise-longue on the verandah, I listened to the talk of those poor people. Their light mockery proved their resignation. They suffered, and—laughed at suffering.

Ah, Mr. Bruel, in your clever, ill-digested compilation you stated, correctly enough, that the province of Ubangi-Shari counted as many as 1,350,000 inhabitants. But you did not say—why didn't you?—that in a certain little village of Ouahm there were, in 1918, only 1080 souls to the 10,000 that had figured in the census seven years before. You spoke of the wealth of that immense region. How is it you failed to remark that famine is queen there?

I know. Yes. What difference does it make to Sirius that in their last extremity ten, twenty, or even a hundred natives went to the dung of the horses, owned by the vultures who dub themselves their benefactors, and hunted for undigested grains of maize or millet to feed upon!

Montesquieu was right when he wrote on a page vibrating with restrained indignation veiled under a surface of cool irony: "They are black from head to foot; their noses are mashed down so flat that it is almost impossible to pity them."

After all if they fall like flies by the thousand and rot in starvation, it is because their country is being "developed." Let them disappear, those who do not adapt themselves to civilization.

Civilization, civilization, pride of the

Europeans and charnel-house of inno-
cents, Rabindranath Tagore, the Hindu
poet, once, at Tokio, told what you were!

You have built your kingdom on
corpses. Whatever you wish, whatever
you do, you move in lies. At sight of
you, gushing tears, shrieks of agony.
You are might prevailing over right.
You are not a torch, you are a conflagra-
tion. You devour whatever you touch.

O my brothers in France, writers of all
parties, honor of the country that has
given me everything, you who often
squabble over a nothing and wantonly
rip each other up, then suddenly become
reconciled when a just and noble cause is
to be championed, I call upon you for
help: I have faith in your big-hearted-
ness.

My book is not a polemic. It comes,
by chance, when its hour strikes. The
Negro question is of the present. Who
made it that? Why, the Americans.
Why, the press campaigns on the other

side of the Rhine. Why, *Romulus Coucou* by Paul Reboux, *Le Visage de la Brousse* by Pierre Bonardi, and *l'Isolement* by that poor fellow Combette. And wasn't it you, *Eve,* you curious little one, who, at the beginning of the year while you were still a daily, carried on an investigation to find out whether a white woman might properly marry a Negro?

Since then, Jean Finot published articles in the *Revue* on the employment of black troops. Since then, Dr. Huot devoted to the Negroes a study in the *Mercure de France.* Since then *Les Lettres* have told of their martyrization in the United States. And in the course of an interpellation in the Chamber of Deputies, Mr. André Lefèvre, Minister of War, was not afraid to say that certain French officials felt they could behave in Alsace-Lorraine restored as if they were in the French Congo.

Such sentiments uttered in such a place .are significant. They prove two things, that people are aware of what is going on in those distant lands and that until now no attempt has been made to remedy the endless abuses, frauds, and atrocities. Moreover, "the best settlers have been, not the professional colonials, but the European troops from the trenches." It is Mr. Diagne who makes this statement.

My brothers in spirit, writers of France, that is only too true. And that is why it behooves you to come forward and declare that from now on, under no pretext, will you have your compatriots who are established in Africa cast discredit upon the nation of which you are the upholders.

Let your voices be heard! It is right and necessary that you come to the aid of those who tell things as they are and not as we should like them to be. And, later, when the colonial Suburas shall have been cleansed, I will describe some of these types. I have sketched a few, but am keeping them a while in my notebooks. I will tell you how, in certain parts, unfortunate Negroes have been obliged to sell their women for as high as seventy-five francs and as low as twenty francs. I will tell you. . . . But I shall speak then in my own name, not in the name of another. It will be my ideas that I shall set forth, not somebody else's ideas. And I know beforehand that the Europeans at whom I shall take aim are so cowardly that not one of them will dare—I know it positively—not one of them will dare to give me the lie in so much as the faintest whisper.

If we knew of what vileness the great colonial life is composed, of what daily vileness, we should talk of it less, we should not talk of it at all. It degrades a man bit by bit. Even among the officials the man who cultivates his mind is a rarity. The colonials haven't got the strength to stand up against the influences of their surroundings. They take to drink. Before the war there were any number of Europeans who could make away with fifteen quarts of Pernod* in a month. Since the war, alack-a-day, I have met one man who beat all records— eighty bottles of whiskey in a month, that was what he could consume drinking steadily.

These and other ignoble excesses reduce those who indulge in them to the last degree of flaccidity. A condition so abject must be a matter of prime concern to those who are charged with representing France, the men who assume responsibility for the evils from which certain parts of the Negro country are at present suffering. But, if they are to be promoted to higher positions, they must have no tales to tell, and so, a prey to ambition, they have renounced pride, they have hesitated, temporized, concealed the truth, woven a tissue of lies. They have not wanted to see, they have not wanted to

* A familiar brand of absinthe in these regions *Translator's note.*

[14]

hear. They are too cowardly to speak out. And so, intellectual anemia joining hands with moral debility, they have deceived their country and felt no remorse.

What I urge upon you to set right is everything embraced in the administration's euphemism of "mistakes." It will be a sharp struggle. You will attack the slave-drivers. Fighting them will be harder than tilting at windmills. Your task is a splendid one. Put your shoulders to the wheel then. Waste no time! It is the will of France.

*   *   *   *   *   *   *   *

The scene of this novel is laid in Ubangi-Shari, one of the four colonies comprising the French Congo, or French Equatorial Africa. It is bounded on the south by the Ubangi River, on the east by the watershed of the Congo and the Nile, on the north and west by the watershed of the Congo and the Shari. Like the other colonies in the group it is divided into departments, which in turn are subdivided into smaller districts. The department is an administrative unit.

The department of the Kemo is one of the most important in Ubangi-Shari. If the famous railway were ever started, the railway they are forever talking about but never getting at, Fort-Sibut, the chief town in the department, might become the capital.

The department of Kemo comprises four districts: Fort-de-Possel, Fort-Sibut, Dakoa, and Grimari. The natives— and even the Europeans—know them only as Kemo, Krebedge, Kombele, and Bembe. Fort-Sibut, otherwise Krebedge, is situated about 190 kilometers north of Bangui, capital of Ubangi-Shari, the European population of which has never exceeded 150 persons.

The district of Grimari (or Bembe or Kandjia from the two names of the river near which the government station is established) is about 120 kilometers east of Krebedge. This region used to be very rich in rubber and had a large population. It was covered with plantations of every kind and teemed with goats and poultry.

Seven years have been enough to work complete ruin. Villages have grown fewer and farther between, the plantations have disappeared, the goats and poultry have been exterminated. As for the natives, they were broken down by incessant toil, for which they were not paid, and were robbed of even the time to sow their crops. They saw disease come and take up its abode with them, saw famine stalk their land, saw their numbers grow less and less.

And yet they are descended from a hardy, warlike tribe, inured to illness and fatigue. Neither raids by the Snoussi nor perpetual internal dissensions could destroy them. Their family name was a guarantee of their vitality. Were they not Bandas? And doesn't Bandas mean nets? For it is with nets that the tribe hunts in the season when the whole horizon is ablaze with the brush* on fire.

Civilization passed that way. And the Dacpas, Dakouas, M'bis, Maroubas, Langbassis, Sabangas and N'gapus, all the Banda tribes were decimated.

The district of Grimari is fertile, picturesque and full of game. Buffalos and wart-hogs abound, as well as guinea-fowl, partridges, and turtle-doves.

Every part of the district is watered by streams. The trees are sparse and stunted; which is not surprising because the equatorial forests stop at Bangui. Fine trees are not to be seen except in the wooded strips bordering the watercourses.

The rivers wind between heights that the Bandas call kagas. The three kagas

---

* The French word *brousse* may be variously translated "bush," "scrub," "brush." In this book only "brush" has been used. The region is a bush or scrub country, but *brousse* as employed in *Batouala* conveys, in addition, the idea of all wild vegetation.—*Translator's note.*

nearest to Grimari are Kossegamba, Gobo, and Biga. The first is two or three kilometers to the southeast of the government station and limits the valley of the Bembe. The other two are in the N'gapu country, twenty kilometers to the northeast.

Such in brief description, is the region in which the scene of this novel of impersonal observation will be laid.

And now, as Verlaine said at the end of the prefatory verses of his *Poèmes saturniens:*

"Go, my book, whither chance may lead you."

R. M.

BORDEAUX, *November 5, 1920.*

BATOUALA

CHAPTER I

IN the course of the night the fire, which it is the custom to kindle every evening, had slowly burned down into a large heap of cinders that still retained some heat.

The circular wall of the hut sweated. A vague light filtered through the opening which served as a door   Under the thatch sounded the steady, delicate rummaging of the white ants, which, under cover of their corridors built of brown earth, had made their way into the branchwork of the low roof, for shelter against the sun and the wet.

Outside the cocks crowed. Their crowing mingled with the bleating of the goats

for the ewes, with the cackling of the hornbills, and—from farther away, from the
depths of the high thickets bordering the
Pombo and the Bembe Rivers—with the
hoarse call of the bacouyas, monkeys with
elongated muzzles like dogs.

Daylight broke.

Although heavy with sleep still, Batouala—Batouala the mokoundji, chief of so
many villages—was quite conscious of
these sounds.

He yawned, shivered, and stretched
himself. Should he go to sleep again?
Should he get up? He did not know.

Get up, N'Gakoura!* Why get up?
He did not even wish to know why. That
there were exceedingly simple decisions
and exceedingly complex decisions to
make—this he scorned.

Now, merely to get up—didn't that re-
quire an enormous effort? In itself a per-
fectly simple decision, so it seemed. As

* "N'Gakoura" corresponds somewhat to "deity." The
natives' idea of N'Gakoura comes out clearly in the
course of the book.—*Translator's note.*

a matter of fact, it was hard; for getting up and working were one and the same thing, at least to the whites.

Not that work dismayed Batouala. He was vigorous, strong-limbed, a splendid walker, more than a match for any man in running, wrestling, and hurling the javelin and the throwing knife.

From one end to the other of the vast Dar Banda his prowess had become a legend. Tradition had already invested his exploits in love and war, his agility and valor in hunting with the glamour of the miraculous. And when Ipeu, the moon, rose in the sky, then the M'bis, Dacpas, Dakouas and Langbassis in their distant villages chanted the valiant deeds of the great mokoundji Batouala to the tom-tom of the li'nghas and the discords of the balafons and koundes.

So work had no terrors for him.

Only, in the language of the whites, work took on a very strange meaning. It meant getting tired without achieving im-

mediate or tangible results, it meant
trouble, annoyance, suffering, the squan-
dering of health, the pursuit of imaginary
ends.

Ah, the whites! They would do better
to go back home, all of them. They would
do better to confine their desires to their
own households and to the cultivation of
their own land, instead of setting their
wishes upon the acquisition of stupid
money.

Life is short. Work is for those who
will never understand life. Doing nothing does not degrade a man. In the eyes
of one who sees things truly, it differs
from laziness.

As for him, Batouala, until it was
proved to the contrary, he would believe
that to do nothing was simply to profit
by everything that surrounds us. To live
from day to day, without thought of yes-
terday or care for the morrow, without
looking ahead—that was perfect.

Really, why get up? Sitting was better than standing, lying down was better than sitting.

The mat on which he slept smelled sweetly of dried grass, and was more softly yielding than the hide of a fresh-killed buffalo.

So, instead of lying there with closed eyes dreaming, why not try to go to sleep again? That would give him the chance to enjoy in full the soft perfection of his bogbo (mat).

First he would have to revive the fire.

A few dry twigs and a little straw would do. He blew, cheeks puffed, on the smouldering sparks. The smoke sent up its spirals, pungent, suffocating. There was a crackling, the flames burst forth, warmth invaded the place.

Now, with his back to the fire, he could just fall asleep again stretched out like a wart-hog, he could just bask in the glow like a lizard in the sunshine. He could imitate the yassi with whom he had been living so long.

She set an excellent example. She lay there peacefully, her head resting on a log, naked, her hands on her belly. She uttered gologolo—snored, to speak plainly! —with her side to a fire that had also burned down to ashes.

What a sound sleep! Sometimes she fumbled at her breasts—wrinkled, flabby breasts like dried tobacco leaves—and scratched herself with long-drawn sighs. Her lips moved. She made half-finished gestures. Then she calmed down again and—snored her even snoring.

In a nook behind the fagots, raised above the chickens, ducks and goats, slept Djouma, the sorry little yellow cur. He slept curled up, head to tail, on a pile of rubber baskets.

All that was visible of his emaciated body were his ears, standing straight up, pointed, mobile. Every now and then, tickled by a flea or stung by a tick, he would shake them. Occasionally, without stirring, he would growl—growl

harder than Yassiguindja, the favorite
yassi of her master, Batouala, the
chieftain. And sometimes, dreaming
dog's dreams, he would inveigh against
the silence with a stifled whff, whff! and
would open his jaws to snap at the void.

Batouala raised himself and leaned on
his elbow. There was no use trying to
sleep any more. Everything was in
league against him. The mist drizzled in
through the entrance to the hut. It was
cold. He was hungry. And the day was
coming on.

How could he possibly sleep? And
where? Outside in the damp thickets
bull-frogs and tree-toads croaked in com-
petition. Inside, in spite of the cold,
mosquitoes and fourous buzz-buzzed.
That was because the fire had gone out
and there was no smoke to stupefy them.
And though the goats had left at cock-
crow, the chickens still were there making
a great to-do.

Even the ducks, the placid ducks,

ranged round their leader, joined in the racket. They stretched their necks to the left and drew them in to stretch them again, lowered them, raised them and quacked, all together, quack-quacked, as if in astonishment.

It was as though something extraordinary had happened, more extraordinary, than anything known to ducks. They wiggled their tails, quacked, looked to the right, looked to the left, with the air of questioning each other.

When they thought they had found what they were looking for, they formed single file by order of their size and marched around the pile of rubber baskets, serious, important, clumsy, all the while repeating their gestures.

At each step in the waddling promenade the weight of their necks pitched them a little forward.

Honk-honk, they went to hold council in a corner. Every few moments they, cast worried looks at the entrance.

Suddenly one of them made up its mind. It took five or six steps toward the spot where the daylight was showing white. In a flurry of alarm it beat the ground with its wings, so as to rush itself along, made a dash at the entrance, disappeared.

Forthwith the others followed its example.

And now Djouma woke up, the sorry little yellow cur. Not that the noise bothered him. He had been accustomed to the noise for many moons.

Even when his mother was alive—his masters had eaten her—every morning had brought the same hubbub.

Men and beasts too often had to sleep together under the same roof. It would be difficult to make any other arrangement.

No help for it. From the very start life had been hard. Djouma was so ignorant of his job of dog that he forgot to bark at each newcomer.

He had to suffer ill-treatment from Batouala and endure the repulses of Yassiguindja. The tricky hostility of the goats combined with the scared flutter and fuss of the fowl had almost maddened him.

Now, as a consequence, he was surly enough. At the least provocation he was all defiance, unless he turned tail and fled. The sight of a white man or the chechia* of a tourougou† sent him scampering into the thicket, to so keen a degree had the fear of kicks sharpened his intelligence.

So, when he woke up it was not because he had been disturbed. Nor was it that he was tired of having slept too much.

There is no such thing as sleeping too much. In this regard he shared the views of his master, Batouala.

He woke up because it was absolutely necessary for him to wake up.

* A cap like those worn by Zouaves.—*Translator's note.*
† A native gendarme.—*Translator's note.*

In the life of a mokoundji, as in the life of any man, a dog counts for no more than the neighings of an m'barta (horse).

A dog! You beat it, you eat it, you castrate it. You have its ears cut. What good is it? Isn't it less than nothing? Once a year, at the season of the brush fires, it makes itself a little bit useful. It excels in the pursuit of dislodged game. But outside of that, it is useless and you pay no attention to it.

The time was well past since anything in the nature of man was left unknown to Djouma, the little yellow cur Long, long before he had learned that if he took it easy and slept late, no one brought him anything to eat.

That is why he got up. Didn't he know that dawn was the time to gulp down the droppings of the kids? They still tasted of milk then. A rich meal, all the more delicious to a dog who has nothing else to take between his teeth.

Droppings! He'd surely find some. It was still too cool for the dung-beetles to have got at their work. Joy! If fortune favored he might even, in the course of his wanderings, come across guinea-hen's eggs in a nest. However, no use counting too much on that.

Djouma rose to his feet, licked his belly and his paws, sneezed violently, hunted for fleas. Then, with his tail between his legs, his nose to the ground, cowed, wretched, he tottered to the entrance.

Having learned to conceal his least feelings, he put on an air of weariness, of utter boredom. Any signs of liveliness would have brought Batouala after him. And that was exactly what must not happen. Otherwise, good-by to the booty that he was sometimes lucky enough to scent out.

Batouala was thinking. Djouma, the

chickens, the ducks, the goats had all left. He felt he ought to follow their example. Besides, there was the ceremony of the circumcision. He had not yet invited anyone. It was time he made up for this omission.

When he had rubbed his eyes with the back of his hand and blown his nose through his fingers, he got up and scratched himself. He scratched his armpits, he scratched his thighs, his head, his buttocks, his arms.

Scratching is a splendid exercise. It sets the blood in circulation. It is a pleasure, and it also points to something. One only needed to look about. All living creatures scratched themselves on waking. It was a good example to follow, since a natural one. It is a bad waking up for a man who doesn't scratch himself.

'But, if scratching was good, yawning was still better. It was a means of chasing sleep away through the mouth.

This supernatural manifestation was easy to account for. In the cold days, didn't everybody breathe out a sort of smoke? Which proves, among other things, that sleep is only a sort of private fire. He, Batouala, was sure of it. A sorcerer was infallible. And since his old father had transmitted his powers to him, he was a sorcerer, he was N'Gakoura.

Besides, how about this! If sleep was not an inner fire, where could the smoke come from? Who had seen smoke without fire? If someone wanted to contradict him in this, he'd certainly have to produce remarkable arguments.

Here a yawn, there a scratch—movements of only trivial importance. Continuing to yawn and scratch, Batouala belched noisily, an old custom that had come to him from his parents, who, in turn, had inherited it from their parents.

The ancient customs were the best.

They could not be too carefully observed. They were founded on experience.

So thought Batouala. He was the keeper of the customs that had fallen into disuse, he remained faithful to the legacy of his forefathers.

He delved no deeper than that. Against custom all reasoning was useless.

Yes. In a little while he would let his friends know when and where to proceed to the ceremony of the circumcision.

For the moment he was content to revive the fire that might have warmed his sleep. Yassiguindja, when she woke up, would only have to attend to her fire. One lived only for oneself, not for another.

At least, so he had been taught.

That done, he went out.

He was not slow getting back. As always, whether dry season or rainy sea-

son, he wore nothing but a loin-cloth.
And it was a cold morning.

There was a heavy fog, so heavy that
he could not even glimpse the huts where
his other eight wives and their children
slept.

Brr! He crouched and crossed his
arms, he shivered, his eyes were red, his
teeth chattered. Ah, the kindly heat of
the fire soon took the numbness from his
stiffened limbs.

Holding his hands to the flames, he
hummed the air of a celebrated song. As
he went along, he improvised the words.
There was a good deal in them about white
"commandants" and women.

The word yassi recurring frequently in
the refrain, he thought of his own Yassiguindja, and went to her as he did every
morning on rising.

The wind was driving the fog from the
horizon where the sun rose to the horizon
where the sun set. The mists had laid
their white waist-cloths round the tops of

the kagas, which were only dimly visible;
and, shrouded in mist, the birds sang, the
parrots, glossy starlings, wagtails, grenadier weavers, and hornbills.

The turtle-doves grazed the ground as
they flew, and the hens, as soon as they
caught sight, through the dissolving mists,
of the kites wheeling low overhead,
scuttled to shelter, heads under wings.

The fresh breeze came and went, came
and went. And the thousands of wet
leaves on the trees rustled. The tops of
the varas tossed to and fro. The bamboos
groaned with the swaying of their long,
flexible stalks.

A last puff of wind tore away the last
shreds of fog, and the sun emerged intact,
washed clean, clear.

A lull came with the widening wound
from the red sun over there, and passed
from space to space, reaching the furthest
solitudes.

But Batouala, the mokoundji, indifferent to the boon of the sunshine, sat beside

the fire he had just kindled a few feet from his hut, untroubled in his mind by any thought, and smoked—slowly, steadily, soberly puffed at his good old pipe, his good old garabo.

It was full daytime.

CHAPTER II

HE smoked, in short puffs, blinking his eyes, and every now and then drawing a deep breath followed by a stream of saliva.

He smoked a long time.

The sun. The higher it rose the hotter it got. Although its heat was grateful to him, he was too accustomed to its daily ardor to give it any thought.

He smoked.

The wind whipped the foliage of the silk-cotton trees, sneaked between the branches, and rustled among the tender-green young shoots.

The rising sap had swelled the trunks into blotches on the living, crackled bark which sweated an amber gum.

The lianas, swung like bridges from tree to tree, coiled and uncoiled their serpentine length.

The wind was laden with the persistent smell of warm earth, trees, and heavy vegetation, the miasma from the small lakes, the spicy aroma of the wild mint.

It was a riot of vegetation. The birds called in bewildered rapture. High up in the air the kites volplaned, black against the blue, faintly uttering their wail of a cry.

On the other side of the Pombo, or on the other side of the Bembe, someone was singing:

"Ey-hey—yaha—ho!"

They must be working there, since song was the invariable accompaniment to labor.

The monotonous chant disturbed the pervading tranquillity. When it stopped, nothing was audible save the crackling of the sun-scorched brush, all the tiny sounds that make up silence.

The song began again, yonder, not so distinct. . . .

Yassiguindja had now prepared manioc, their usual fare, and had also boiled some sweet potatoes and wild purslane, each in separate pots.

When her man deigned to come and eat, she took up the pipe, and in her turn puffed at it, in the meanwhile attending distractedly to the grilling of some caterpillars.

Her eight companions sat leaning, each against her own hut, and proceeded to perform their toilet.

It was an unaffected business. Man and woman are made for one another. Since they cannot be ignorant of their differences, why be ashamed? Shame of the body is silly. Modesty is just another one of the hypocrisies of the whites. Only defects or malformations should be concealed. Men and women hide what they have only when they know it is ridiculous or unfit.

Batouala went from the manioc to the caterpillars, from the caterpillars to the sweet potatoes.

Between every two or three mouthfuls he gulped one or two copes of kéné, a beer made of fermented millet.

When he had had his fill, he indicated by a gesture to Yassiguindja that he wanted his pipe again.

And once more he smoked, a long, long smoke, in short puffs punctuated by deep respirations.

Finally, content with having spent the first part of the day so well, he began to examine the toes of his left foot.

He was hunting for jiggers.

Jiggers. Indeed a poor Negro had better hunt for jiggers. If not, the little pests were liable to deposit anywhere on one's body more eggs than there were women in an inhabited village.

Not so with the whites. Suppose a jigger got at their skin? They were so tender, they noticed it instantly and didn't feel right again until a boy had caught and killed it.

But what was the use of dwelling on

this? It was well known: the whites were not so hardy as the blacks.

An example—one in a thousand? Under pretext of getting the tax that way, they forced all the Negroes they thought made good teams to transport tremendous loads. The journeys lasted three, four, five days. Little cared they what the sandoukous* weighed. What difference did the rain or the heat make to them? *They* did not suffer. What if the hardships from weather and insect pests fell upon the Negroes! The whites were under cover. Did you understand now?

The whites, ah, the whites!

They fretted and fumed against mosquito bites. The fourous annoyed them. The buzzing of flies made them nervous They were afraid of the scorpions, those black, venomous prakongos who live in decayed roofing, or among

* "Sandoukou" means "trunk," "box"; in this case, presumably, boxes filled with rubber.—*Translator's note.*

small stones, or rubbish. They dreaded
spiders. Everything alarmed them.
Ought a man worthy of the name bother
about what lives and goes on around him?
Ah, the whites, the whites!

Their feet? A stench. And why box
feet up in black, white, or yellow hides?

If it were only their feet that stank.
Bah, their whole bodies gave out the smell
of a corpse.

That people should bag their feet in
sewed skin—well, all right. But to shield
one's eyes with glass—white, blue, black,
yellow glass! To cover one's head with a
little basket! N'Gakoura, that passed
understanding.

In sudden contempt Batouala shrugged
his shoulders. To give expression to his
feelings he spat out.

Ah, the whites! Their meanness, their
knowledge of everything, that was what
made them so fearful.

Some of them, those from France,
brought over machines which, at the turn-

ing of a bit of wood, spoke like live whites, one didn't know why or how.

Others—yes, he had seen it—others swallowed knives whole.

It was a fact, not to be disputed. Throughout the country, and beyond, everyone knew the terrible Moro-Kamba, the sword-eating commandant who had pacified the Bandas.

Then there were some who, sitting in their chairs, could look through glass in a tube and see the country far, far away as though it were right before them, and could watch what was going on at an immense distance.

Amazing, eh?

And that doctorro—doctorro was the name by which the whites called their sorcerer—who made you urinate blue—yes, blue!—if such was his pleasure.

But here was the most terrifying thing of all.

A few days ago when the new commandant arrived, hadn't Batouala seen him remove the skin from his hand, a skin that only slightly resembled other known skins, but a skin nevertheless?

He had peeled it off, and it had not hurt him. If it had hurt him, he would have screamed. Not having screamed, it had not hurt him.

Besides all this, wasn't it said that certain ones among them had the privilege of removing their teeth or taking out one of their eyes and putting it, tooth or eye, down on the table, right there, in front of everybody!

Umm! Never could the Negro sorcerers achieve such things. Bit by bit contempt yielded to mingled terror and admiration.

The sun had reached the zenith.

The glossy starlings, as usual, proclaimed the news The shrilling of the cicadas had not yet begun to torment space. Everything seemed to sleep an immense smothered sleep. Except for three strong gusts of wind which always blew at this time of the day. Then followed the caress of no breeze. It awoke no undulations in the giant plants, and the leaves of the silk-cotton trees were as motionless as the smoke—off there in the distance.

Now the cicadas set up their strumming.

This was the hour that the Negroes chose for work.

Batouala started off to an elevation dominating the level country around. There were three li'nghas there of different sizes.

He went up to the largest of these hollow shells of wood, picked up two mallets lying on the ground, and struck two blows in slow succession. They rang out sonorous in the motionless air.

A great silence followed. It was broken again by two more, shorter blows. After which came a fanfare of rub-a-dubdubs, more and more violent, faster and

[47]

faster, more and more urgent, then slow
and lingering, and ending on the smallest
li'ngha in a rapid decrescendo, with one
strong final bang of summons.

And behold, over there, over there, farther away, still farther away, from everywhere, from the right, from the left, from
behind and in front, the same noises came
responsive, the same rumblings, the same
beatings on li'nghas; some weak, hesitat-
ing, muffled, indistinct; others clear and
re-echoing from kaga to kaga. The invisible broke into life.

"You have summoned us," said these
sounds, "you have summoned us. We
have heard you. We listen to you. What
do you wish? Speak."

Twice space repeated the same notes,
confused or distinct.

When the horizon had absorbed the last
quaver, Batouala replied.

There was no force in his first words.
They suggested rather the monotonous
torpor of the days, the solitude that noth-

ing either saddens or enlivens, the resignation to fate.

The mallets struck the three li'nghas alternately. A melody arose from them, oppressive as the weather preceding a tornado before the donvorro begins to blow.

The song brightened up. There was a sudden stop, then it began again, and swelled, and rose, always rose, higher and higher.

Batouala streamed with sweat. He was happy, he almost danced.

His men, their women, their children, their friends, the friends of their friends, the chiefs whose blood he had drunk, who had drunk his blood—he invited them, all of them. In nine days they were to come to the grand yangba that he was going to give on the occasion of the ga'nza.

The jerks of sound from Batouala's li'nghas, which had been expected since many rainy seasons, promised wonders. There would be things to eat and drink, there would be palavers, there would be amusement. Above all there would be yangba. Not one yangba, but all the yangbas. Not only the elephant's step, the dance of the javelins, and the dance of the warriors, but also, *also,* above all, the dance of love, the dance that the Sabangas danced so well.

There would be things to eat and drink, there would be yangba, yangba. Ah, the manioc, the potatoes, the dazos, the gourds, the yams, the maize! Ah, the millet beer, the vékés, the pimentos, the honey, the fish, and the alligator's eggs! All that there would be to eat, all that, and much more. All that there would be to drink, all that and much more. They'd eat and drink to the sound of the oliphants and balafons. They were invited to come. Yes, yes, yes! It was the festivity of the ga'nzas. Circumcision and excision took place only once in a twelvemonth. They must come. How they'd laugh, yabao!*

* "Yabao" is merely an exclamation.—*Translator's note.*

The echoes leapt with mirth. They leapt with the mirth of his speech, they prolonged his pleasantries, they rolled out his laughter.

He stopped. A heavy expectancy freighted the air. Not for long. All around, from far away, very far away, the conversation began again, on the invisible tom-toms. And distant though the instruments were, one caught, at the end of each phrase, the same notes of secret joy.

"We listened.   We heard you and understood. . . . You are the greatest of M'bis, Batouala. . . . You are the greatest of mokoundjis. . . . We'll come. . . . Certainly we'll come. . . . And our friends will come. . . . We shall enjoy ourselves.   The carousal! . . . We shall sing. We shall dance. . . . We shall drink like fish . . . like the whites! You can count on me. . . . Porro. . . . Ouorro. . . . Kanga. . . . Yabingui. . . . Delepou. . Tougoumali. . . . Yabada   All the

M'bis and all the N'gapus will come.
We'll come. . . . We'll come. . . ."

The last response died away on the horizon.

Batouala went down to the junction of
the Bembe and Pombo Rivers, to examine a fish-net he had laid there.

He carried two javelins, a bow, and a
wallet of goat-skin.

Wherever one went, no matter how
short a way, one should never forget to
take a wallet along. One could hide so
many things in it.

He filled it with a few bi'mbi leaves, a
quiver of barbed arrows, and several
loaves of manioc bread.

That was all he needed, no more and
no less. Whatever turned up in the way
of a danger, he was prepared. Was he
not equipped with his javelins, his bow
and arrows? Against hunger, there was
his manioc bread. Thanks to the bi'mbi
leaves he could even enrich his fare. All

he need do was immerse the leaves in the fish-net, and they'd stupefy every fish that ventured in.

He started off.

He looked up at the sun as he walked —one of the numerous habits bequeathed him by his parents. The older he grew the more he appreciated their excellence.

The whites didn't seem to understand the use of knowing where to set one's foot. One cut oneself on stones and slipped in the mud. With a little bit of care one could avoid cuts and falls, at least make them less severe. There was no loss of time involved, not to the man who knew how to husband his efforts. Besides, experience taught one that time had no value; one simply trusted to one's wisdom.

Soon after Batouala left, Bissibingui arrived.

He was a handsome young man, strong, well-built. He always found something

to eat at Batouala's home, and a bogbo
to sleep on. For Batouala honored him
with his particular esteem. Nor was the
great mokoundji the only one to cherish
an affection for Bissibingui. Of Batouala's nine wives eight, without his knowledge, had testified to the warmth of their
friendship to Bissibingui.

As for Yassiguindja she was already
less obedient to the orders of the man who
had purchased her than to the orders of
Bissibingui, and she only awaited a favorable occasion to show how greatly she
craved him.

A woman must never refuse a man's
desire. Neither must a man refuse a
woman's desire. The sole law was instinct. To deceive your husband, to belong to him alone, neither the one nor the
other was of much importance.

If one used the property of the habitual
possessor, one compensated him in poultry, goats or waist-cloths. And everything was for the best.

Not so, unfortunately, with Batouala. He was jealous, vengeful, violent; he'd certainly not hesitate to do away with the man who poached on his preserves. He wanted to be the only one to plant the seed in his women, whom he had acquired at the cost of heavy sacrifices. Yassiguindja, Batouala's favorite, was well aware of this, and was not ready to give herself until there was absolutely no risk of discovery.

For the past two or three months Bissingui had come at regular intervals. He was in his sixteenth season of rains, the age at which males worthy of the name run after women from morning to evening, like panthers after antelopes.

Of a sudden his body had developed, he had taken on muscle and weight. It was the yassis who sought him out, not he them. They sang his praises; they praised him for his manly vigor, his fire. He was their favorite. He had been party to breaches between many a couple.

Whence interminable palavers. Time
and again the commandant, wearied with
complaints, had threatened him with
prison.

That had added to his reputation.

His coming was greeted with cries of
joy. The women asked him what women
he had been with since the last time they
had seen him; whether it was true about
such and such a one. They brought up a
thousand intimate details.

He smiled, without replying to their
pleasantries, took up Batouala's garabo,
stuffed it with the n'gao leaves, and
lighted it with an ember from the fire.

That done, he stretched out on a mat
and smoked, in short puffs, blinking his
eyes.

"You should pay attention to the
women you choose," said Yassiguindja.
"Some day you'll come back rich with a
good kassirri."

The eight other women laughed.

"E-hee! E-hee! . . . E-e-e-e-! . . .

Yabao, that Yassiguindja! E-e-e-e!"

They slapped their thighs.

"But the kassirri is nothing," Yassiguindja went on. "It'll be different, Bissibingui, if you catch something worse. Iche! You'll disappear by bits, tiny, tiny bits. But first you'll be covered with sores, spotted like a panther. Later you'll lose your teeth, your hair, your fingers. Think of Yakeulepeu who died—three, four, five moons ago."

The women laughed harder.

Their laughter kept up until Batouala returned.

They told him what they were laughing about.

He joked, too. The fun rose to a higher pitch. They held their sides, they plumped up and down on the ground, they wept.

"E-hee! E-e-e-e! . . . That Batouala, N'Gakoura!"

The sun was setting.

The cooing of the golokotos (turtle-doves), the scolding of the grenadier weavers, the wail of the wagtails and kites gradually ceased.

Mists as fine as cobwebs veiled the tops of the kagas. The sun sank. The chickens, ducks and goats went to shelter again.

Clouds spread and dappled the sky. The sun had almost disappeared. It was so red it looked like a great flaming flower. It shot out rays in widening sheaves. Finally it dropped into the alligator jaws of the void.

Then large beams stained space with blood. Gradually the colors faded, from shade to shade, from transparence to finer transparence, and the beams in the immense sky scattered. The last shades of color were blotted out. The indefinable silence that had watched over the agony and the death of the sun spread over the whole earth.

A poignant melancholy touched the stars, which had appeared in the infinite non-color. The warm earth steamed. The damp smells of the night were coming on. The dew began to weigh upon the brush. The paths were slippery. The faint aroma of wild mint seemed to hum in the wind along with the humming of the dung-beetles.

In the air were the sounds of a mortar and pestle, you couldn't tell where, crushing manioc, millet, or maize; and tomtoms were beating, you couldn't tell where, to enliven yangbas.

In the distance, here and there, fires were kindled. One guessed at the huts and the smoke. Toads, according to their species, piped, or croaked, or shrilled. Djouma, the little yellow dog, barked and barked.

What was this stupor? What was this anguish?

Like a canoe grazing the water-plants —oh, how gently it glided across the clouds!—behold Ipeu, the moon.

It was already six sleeps old.

CHAPTER III

THREE days before the festival of the ga'nzas there was a violent tornado which finished the havoc wrought by a season of disastrous rains.

There had been no warning signs to presage its coming. The day had risen upon Grimari like so many other days, uncertain at first, then warm and sunny.

The wind, gentle, and neither cool nor sultry, had stirred the dense foliage, in the shade of which the golokotos cooed, and the bokoudoubas and the lihouas, which differed from the golokotos, the first only in size, the second only in the green of their plumage.

Above the fields of millet, above the trees and kagas, the kites in growing numbers sailed and wheeled, never tiring.

Occasionally one of them dropped plumb upon its prey, then rose on high again with slow large flappings of its wings, as if paddling the air, and soared into the distance, far, far. . . .

The weather was neither cool nor sultry.

Along the Bembe and the Pombo the monkey-folk amused themselves, the tagouas cutting up their capers, the n'gouhilles making their strange grimaces. The n'gouhilles had fur like a black-and-white waist-cloth, and the tagouas seemed always to be crying, their call sounded so exactly like the imitation of a baby's wail.

The monkeys scampered off in alarm before a swarm of bees, which had started up in pursuit of a honey-eating bird.

For a second one heard nothing but the humming of the bees. The rustle of the leaves in the wind produced the illusion that the bees were flying about on the same spot, but they were already far away.

The weather was neither cool nor sultry.

The bokoudoubas and the golokotos cooed. From the villages hidden on the hills, from the valleys sheltering other villages came monotonous chants and the sound of pestles crushing the dry manioc; while in the motionless sky, the kites wheeled in still greater numbers.

Macoude, the fisherman, came late in the morning to surprise his brother Batouala, whom he saw only rarely. He had found two large fish in his net and had come to invite Batouala to share his meal with him.

Macoude and Batouala, having the same father and mother, were closer kin than a man's children usually were, since any man, if his means allowed, could buy several women and have children by each of them.

Bissibingui, who happened to be there, was also invited.

The three started off, walking single file like ducks.

It was not right to walk side by side. A custom old as the Negro race itself dictated single file.

Djouma, ears down, followed them. . . .

"There are some people who act very proud," said Indouvoura, one of Batouala's wives.

She was jealous and sensual, and it never failed to make her angry to see Bissibingui leave her for Yassiguindja.

"Yes   there are," she continued. "To be sure there are.—Nobody need listen who doesn't want to listen.—But you can't help it: people will assume superior airs, won't they, Yassiguindja?"

General laughter. That was one for Yassiguindja, who was not liked.

"They will, Indouvoura," she replied. "But I don't know whom you're referring to. Probably that N'gapu woman who married a powerful M'bi chief? My goodness, *she's* certainly got no cause to be proud—the low beastly things she gives herself up to. However, I'll excuse her. She was the wife of a white man. That explains everything."

"The bitch! The insulting bitch!" cried Indouvoura. "The way she insults me! The womb of the woman who bore you was rotten. You're filth, you're filth of filth. Don't say a word! Don't you dare to open your mouth, or I'll jump down your throat."

"Why bellow, old dear? I'm not deaf. Shall I tell you a few things about yourself? Ah, yes! Ah, yes!"

"Shall I break this pestle on your dirty face? I'll tell Batouala that you deceive him with Bissibingui. I'll tell him. . . ."

"Yes, yes, yes. I beg pardon, Indouvoura. I've known you so many seasons of the rains that I forgot you were a N'gapu and had been a white man's woman. Need I assure you that I didn't refer to you? Everybody knows how virtuous you are, and no one better than this Bissibingui you mentioned. He knows how you manage to repulse men. . . ."

Indouvoura leapt at Yassiguindja, ready to beat and bite and scratch. Her companions held her back. She poured out threats: she would complain to the commandant, she would tell everybody that Yassiguindja had taken a yorro to keep from having children. She would ask the elders to make her drink poison to prove it. But after all what was there to get so excited about? Bissibingui! Pff! She snapped her fingers at him. One didn't go with a man who had the kassirri!

"When a person can't get what he wants to eat, he says he's not hungry," said Yassiguindja. "And as for that goat, Bissibingui, if he's got what you say he has, I'm sorry for you, my poor dear."

Now the laughs turned against Indouvoura.

"You attacked someone stronger than yourself," she said.

"See what jealousy brings one to, In-douvoura. When you took Bissibingui, was I jealous?"

"Do you think he belongs to no one but you? What an appetite!"

"That Yassiguindja! She's a precious one."

"She always has a ready retort."

"Come on now, come on," she said. "Enough for to-day. Let's rather eat this manioc. A baba, that's nice. Sleeping, eating, manioc bread, men, dancing, to-bacco, they are the only real things."

General merriment greeted this sally.

Little by little the sky had turned an ashen grey, then the color of laterite.

The wind blew up, sudden, sultry. The flies began to buzz, the flies, the flies, everywhere.

One by one the birds fell into silence. One by one the kites disappeared.

Great wan clouds rose from behind the kagas. They came blown at the will of the aerial currents, piling up, gathering in denser and denser masses.

Presently a hidden force drove them toward the Bembe.

They hurried on, blacker than coal, tangled at the edges, jostling, thronging, straddling one another, galloping like buffalos fleeing before the brush fires.

Forked streaks split the whole mass of them. And the echoes rumbled with the detonations of the thunder.

Pots and mats were pulled into the huts. The blue smoke hung stationary over the roofs and encircled the outer walls.

Nothing stirred. The clouds covered the low sky. Now, motionless, they lowered over the Bembe, the Dela, the Deka. They lowered over the villages of Yakidji, Soumana, Yabingui, and Batouala; over the villages of Bandapou, Tamande, Yabada, Gratagba, Oualade, Poumayassi, Pangakoura; over the whole of that green country which the shadow of them was stifling. They suppressed the life of the day, they held an imminent threat, they awaited a signal which did not come. . . .

Yonder, yonder, between Soumana and Yakidji, the dusk of the clouds changed into steel-colored bands that united heaven and earth.

The rain. Driven by the same power as the clouds it fell upon the Bembe, it rushed upon Grimari.

As it came on stronger, it covered the ground it had conquered with spraying mists.

Ouhououou! At last! A great warm gust of wind from no one knew where.

The leaves of the banana-trees dashed against each other. There were confused croakings—the koungbas and the letteureus (frogs and toads) calling to the rain.

A great howl, and the wind came on, brushing the leaves wrong side up, twisting the branches, mauling the lianas, tearing the foliage, sweeping the ground, lifting the red dust. It passed, it fled, it grew weaker. The shriek of it died down, scattered, ceased altogether. Where had it gone to!

Silence again. The troubled silence of the uproar that had turned still.

The wind again. And the rain coming on, on, on. The wind brought the pleasant smell of wet earth. One rumble followed another. The thunder drew nearer and nearer. The rain fell in fine, light, scattered drops that pattered upon the dry rocks and brush. The air turned cooler, the wind rose. The donvorro.

From instant to instant it gained in fury. And the rain came down in floods, in torrents, in warm heavy masses, swift, close, indefatigable, irresistible, incessant. It fell upon the Bembe, it fell upon the Dela, it fell upon the Deka. It fell upon all the kagas that were still visible, upon the whole horizon which was no longer visible   The rain and the donvorro harassed the brush with their combined fury. They stripped the leaves from the trees, broke off branches, snatched away the roofs.

Moisture falling on the vast over-heated tract rose in a heavy, impenetrable vapor that hung low upon the land. Water sought water, gathered and swelled, traced out channels, leapt in cas-cades, and formed into rivulets, which bounded down the slopes into the river.

The donvorro hastened their course. And the rain coming down faster and faster and harder and harder, gutted the roofs, staved them in, poured into the huts, put out the fires, washed down the walls.

The forked lightning leapt. The sharp cracks of thunder, the crash of trees bear-ing down other trees in their fall, the howl-ing of the tempest, shattered the vault of space with the booming of the flood-gates of heaven.

The tornado lasted all day, all night,

and the whole of the next morning until the hour when the sun had just passed the zenith.

The wind gradually died down. The rain, however, continued to fall, but it was light and fine and cool.

From the brush, which in places had been turned into swamps, croaked the koungbas whom the rain delighted —the koungbas and the letteureus croaked.

When the grass is flooded and all the little dips in the ground become pools, the toads and frogs begin to sing.

Bull-frogs, you take the lead. Your voices are a deep, regular bass. Take the lead: the lesser frogs will join in.

The letteureus and koungbas carolled. They were glad of the wet. In wet weather they were really masters of the world.

They sang:

"Ka-ak . . . ka-ak . . . ti-tilu . . . ti-tilu

. . . kee-ex   . kee-ex . . . kide-kidi . . .
ki-kidi .   dja-ah . . . dja-ah. . . ."

Tinkling of cattle-bells, thump of pestles, clank of javelin on javelin, involun-
tary retchings, loud, muffled, harsh, dis-
cordant—the croaking of all sorts of
toads and all sorts of frogs made yangba.
They made an anvil chorus of braying and
bellowing.

"Ti-tilu . . . ti-tilu . . . kee-ex . . . kee-ex
    ka-ak   ka-ak . . . ki-kidi . . . kidi-
kidi. . . ."

It was a deafening tom-tom at the end
of the day.   Suddenly it stopped.   Suddenly it began again.

The rain was no longer falling.   The
paths were slippery.   Ants had abandoned their wrecked hills and were crossing the paths in long lines.   They left in
their wake the lingering smell of decay.

Night fell, with almost no twilight in-
tervening.

Slowly the moon emerged from its hut
of clouds and traversed its plantation of

stars—yellow, shining, not quite round, without a halo. The stars sparkled. That was all there was—the stars, thousands and thousands of stars, and the moon.

A nocturnal bird uttered "Oubou-hou, oubou." The frogs croaked eternally. The cicadas chirped, and the crickets strummed. A few fire-flies, at long intervals, tore the air with their green intermittent light. Everything else slept. It was night. The wind was soft and slow. It was cold.

CHAPTER IV

THE full moon traversed the region of the stars. The festival of the ga'nzas was about to begin.

What a stroke of good fortune! A week before, the commandant had left Grimari on a tour of inspection in the neighborhood of Bamayassi. The billy-goat away, the nanny-goats will play. Swarms of natives overran the grounds of the Government station—the only place that offered room enough for the full sweep of the various figures and the dance of the warriors.

A large empty space, as broad as it was long, reached from the commandant's house down to the Bembe. And only one man had been left in charge, only one native gendarme, one tourougou, Boula, for whom the natives didn't give a tinker's curse—Boula in sole charge of the administration building and annexes, the training-camp, and the guard-house.

Who really did care about a kouloungoulou—the nickname they had given Boula because, they said, he crawled like a milleped.

The ga'nzas not having arrived yet, the yangba was not in full swing, but the indications were that it was going to be wonderful.

A dozen li'nghas scattered about seemed to be waiting expectant These were not ugly little tom-toms, dirty from use, weatherbeaten, worm-eaten. On the contrary, each of them visibly swelled with pride over its double convexity, the great round of an enormous tree-trunk patiently hollowed out. They had been given a pale coat, made of mixed white clay and manioc meal, with a broad band of red running lengthwise and breadthwise.

On the ground were spread baskets of millet, manioc cakes, whole clusters of bananas, dishfuls of caterpillars, eggs, fish, bitter tomatoes, wild asparagus. There were quantities of meats, either sun-dried or grilled over a fire—antelope meat, elephant meat, quarters of wart-hog and buffalo. There were the tubers that the whites despised—dazos, for example, every bit as good as their white potatoes. There were bangaos or sweet potatoes, both the red-skinned and the yellow-skinned sorts. There were baba's-sos or yams. There were great jars brimming over with the drink made of fermented millet or maize. And there were a few bottles of Pernod.

The Pernod had been bought from the boundjoudoulis (white tradesmen) and was reserved for the chiefs, head-men, and elders.

From the numerous fires arose volumes of smoke, black, heavy, and very pungent from the damp wood.

The roads from Kama, Pangakoura, Pouyamba, and Yakidji swarmed with the latecomers hastening toward these fires visible from afar—men, women, children, boys, boyesses, slaves, dogs.

They had come, and still were coming, from their kagas, their thickets, their muddy patas-patas, or their plantations, armed with arrows and javelins, and carrying burning pieces of wood to light their way in the wooded strips through which they had to pass before they reached the small lakes.

The women, as soon as they arrived, set right to work with their koufrou to pound the maize and millet and manioc into meal, and while pestles banged in wooden mortars they sang the song of the kouloungoulou.

The kouloungoulou, as is known, lives in dung.
That's all he eats, too, they say. Think of it!
   Kouloungoulou, kouloungoulou,
   Kouloungoulou, ho! Ia-hey!

His wealth consists of but one thing.
He got it from the boundjou (white man).
And excellent husband that he is,
He passed it to his yassi.

She passed it to their daughter.
> Kouloungoulou, kouloungoulou,
> Kouloungoulou, ho! Ia-hey!

How is it that we saw a kouloungoulo,
Wearing a tourougou's chechia,
Passing through our lovely fields?
Yassis, yassis, take care, beware
Of the filthy kouloungoulou.
He's no friend for you.
> Kouloungoulou, kouloungoulo,
> Kouloungoulu, ho! Ia-hey!

There were bursts of laughter. The merriment became general. They laughed for the sake of laughing. They talked without knowing just what they were going to say: the kéné was already working. They drank maize-beer on top of millet-beer, and drank and drank without cease.

A wonderful gathering! All the M'bis and all the N'gapus were there with their elders.

Batouala and his old parents formed the centre of a group of chiefs and their head-men.

He held forth.

The death of several whites had been reported at Bangui. . . . It was said that the Governor was soon going to Bandor-ro . . . that over in France in M'Pou-tou (Europe) the Frandjes were fighting the Zalemans.

While talking he stuffed the garabos within reach with hemp* and tobacco, lit them, took several puffs, which is the custom, and passed them round.

"You know, Batouala, I have just come back from Krebedge," said Pangakoura, the great Mandjian chief. "One learns a good deal travelling, doesn't one? For example, that the whites don't like each other. Here's proof, absolute proof — I had a complaint to make against a Portuguese, and I went to the commandant, the one we call Kotaya on account of his huge paunch. I told him my story, trimming it up a little, of course.

" 'Pangakoura,' he said, 'you certainly are an idiot, the most idiotic idiot I've

* Contains a strong narcotic.—*Translator's note.*

ever come across. What! you poor old dunderhead, don't you know a Poutriquess doesn't count? Listen. At the beginning of things—you follow me, do you? — at the beginning of things the N'Gakoura of the whites took the best he had on hand and created the whites. Then he gathered together the leavings and created the dirty niggers like you. Much later, he wanted to make the Portuguese and looked about for something to create them from. There was nothing left but the offal of the blacks. Out of that he kneaded the first Portuguese.' "

Volleys of laughter.

"Don't you think that the drop in the price of rubber is an unexpected piece of luck for us?" asked Batouala. "Even if the commandant had been away, we should not, but for this chance, have been able to come here to the Government grounds to warm our livers. There would have been one of those wretched boundjoudoulis on the spot to make us pay a pata, yes, five francs, for what the whites wouldn't have to pay more than a meya, , ten sous."

"Your words are like clear water," said Yakidji. "We must give thanks to N'Gakoura. All the traders, on account of this happy crisis, have had to go back to Krebedge or Bangui. May they rot to death, their mouths open, their feet in filth."

"And that isn't all. Oh, that isn't all, Batouala," said Yabada. "On account of the grand palavers between the white Zalemans and the white Frandjes, the yongorogombes are going to be shipped to M'Poutou. Yes, they're all going off to war at M'Poutou, all the long muskets,* all the black soldier-trash. Probably our present masters will join them. I myself think they will."

"Yabao!" quavered Batouala's old father, "as sure as my hairs are white, I

---

* "Long muskets" is the nickname for black troops not native to Ubangi-Shari, but brought by the French from the coast and other districts.—*Translator's note.*

think you're taking kagas for rivers and
your wishes for the reality. Soon it will
be three seasons of rains since the Frandjes and the Zalemans have been palaver-
ing. Have the Frandjes given any sign
of wanting to leave? Not a bit. There's
danger over there. Why should they go
there to get killed? Each man looks out
for his own skin, Yabada."

Louder laughter.

"You're always right, elder. I admit
it. But will you allow me to hope that
the Zalemans will lick the Frandjes?"

"Ah, you boundoua Yabada! Zalemans
—Frandjes: whites all the same. Why
change one for the other? We are under
the Frandjes, we know their good qualities and their bad qualities. They play
with us like a niaou with a mouse. In the
end the niaou always eats the mouse with
which it has played. Since sooner or later
we're going to be killed and eaten, what
use is there to wish for different niaous
than those we have? It's like escaping

buffalos to fall into the clutches of a lurking panther."

The discussion became general.

"He's right. Why change? The new ones might be worse."

"They don't like us. And we pay them back in their own coin."

"We ought to murder them."

"We ought."

"We will some day, later on."

"When the Banziris, Goubous, Yako-mas, Sabangas, Dacpas, all, in short, who talk the Banda or the Mandjia or the Sango language, stop their old quarrels."

"That will be when the Bembe flows backward."

"And Macoude catches the moon in his nets."

Laughter again, so long and loud that one scarcely heard a great noise that sounded in the distance.

"Or you are all sons of a dog," cried Batouala under the influence of pipe and drink. "Or else you are all drunker than

I am. Are you men, yes or no? Have
the bazi'nguers of Snoussi castrated you?
I don't know. At any rate I for my part
can't help cursing the whites. I remember the time when the M'bis lived peacefully along the Niou-Bangui, between
Bessou-Kemo and Kemo-Ouadda. As
soon as the first whites appeared, the most
of us picked up our fetishes, our pots,
poultry, mats, dogs, women, goats, children, ducks, and withdrew to the country
near Krebedge.

"I was very little then.

"There were struggles; there were huts
to build and fields to sow. All useless.
The whites settled at Krebedge.

"Another move. We liked Griko. We
halted at Griko. The same difficulties getting established there; but we thought
we'd be able to draw a peaceful breath.
Wrong! The whites—the whites again!
—descended on Griko.

"We started off once more. To Grimari. There was a fine location for us in

Grimari between the Bembe and the Pombo. We settled there. Alas! before we had completed our building and planting the whites were upon us again. By that time we were worn out and discouraged. Besides, we had lost so many men taking land away from others by force that we were afraid our tribe might be destroyed. So we stayed where we were, and—looked pleasant. "

The great noise in the distance drew nearer.

"No use. Our submissiveness didn't bring us the good will of the whites. Not content with trying to suppress our customs, they wanted to impose theirs on us. We had no right to play patara for money. We had no right to get drunk. Our singing and dancing interfered with their sleep. But—pay them a tithe, and they'd deign to put up with our singing and dancing. Pay, pay, pay, always pay! The Government treasuries are insatiable.

"Yet after all, we'd give into them, the

mean bullies, if only they applied the same
logic to themselves that they do to us.
They don't. Listen. Two moons ago that
beast Ouorro, drunk as a white man, beat
up one of his yassis. She was bruised and
swollen from head to foot. Blame him if
you feel like it. But who of you—eh?—
has never beaten his yassi?

"The jade actually went to the commandant to complain. It so happened
that he had several white guests stopping
with him. As a rule, he is that rare thing
among the whites—sober. On this occasion he was full to toppling over. He
ordered a tourougou to place Ouorro under arrest. The tourougou carried out his
orders rather gently, and the commandant
went into a fury and threw an empty bot-
tle at his head. The tourougou fell down,
the blood streamed from his forehead. He
made a face from the pain, and all the
whites laughed as though it were a huge
joke. That's the way they treat us.

"Yabada, see for yourself. Dare to

risk two francs at patara under the eyes of the commandant. What'll you get for the awful crime? A lashing with a knotted whip, and with that you'll come off easy. Only the whites may play games of chance."

Batouala's eyes were bloodshot, he shouted and stammered.

"The whites are good for nothing. They call us liars, and treat us accordingly. Our lies don't deceive anyone. If we embellish the truth sometimes, it's because the truth isn't good enough; manioc without salt is tasteless. But the whites! They lie for nothing. They lie with method. They lie by rote, as naturally as they breathe. That's what gives them the advantage over us.

"They say the Negroes under one chief hate the Negroes under another chief. La, la! How about the boundjoudoulis, the long muskets, the Mon Pères (priests), and the commandants? Do they agree? And if they don't why should we? A man's a man, no matter what his color, here as well as in M'Poutou. "

The huge sound in the distance had become more distinct, like the droning of thousands of blue or green voumas (flies) about a carcass.

Batouala rose to his feet, and shouted and gesticulated.

"I will never allow anyone to deny the meanness of the whites. What I blame them most for is their lying and their cheating. The things they didn't promise us! 'Later on,' they said, 'you'll see, it's only for your own good that we force you to work. We'll take only a very, very small part of the money we make you earn. We'll use what we take to build villages for you, roads, bridges, machines that run on iron rails by means of fire.'

"Where are they—the roads, the bridges, the wonderful machines? Where I ask. Nowhere! Not a sign of them. Nothing, nothing! And so far from taking only a tiny part of what we earn, they rob us of our last sou. Aren't we to be pitied? I ask you, aren't we to be pitied?

"Thirty moons ago we got three francs a kilo for our rubber. Over night the price went down. Without offering the shadow of an explanation, they paid us only fifteen sous for the same quantity of banga—one meya and five bi'mbas. And the Governor chose that very moment to raise our tax from five to seven and ten francs.

"Now there isn't anybody who doesn't know that from the first day of the dry season to the last day of the rainy season we work just to swell the taxes—if not also to fill the pockets of our commandants.

"We're nothing but flesh to feed the taxes. We're nothing but beasts of burden. Beasts? Not even that. Dogs? They feed their dogs, and tend their horses. We? We're less than their animals, we're the lowest of the low. They're killing us by slow degrees. . . ."

A drunken crowd pressed up behind the
group of which Batouala was the centre.

They reviled the whites. Batouala was
right, a thousand times right. Of old,
before the coming of the whites, they had
lived happily. They had worked a little,
for themselves, they had eaten and drunk
and slept. From time to time they had
had bloody palavers and had plucked the
livers from the dead to eat their courage,
and incorporate it in themselves. Such
had been the happy days of old, before the
coming of the whites.

Now they were mere slaves. There
was nothing to be hoped for from a heartless race. For the boundjous (whites)
were heartless. They deserted their children by negro women, and these children,
knowing they had sprung from the
whites, scorned to associate with the
blacks. They were full of hate and envy,
these boundjouvoukos, these half-whites-
half-blacks. They were lazy, mischievous,
rotten with vices.

As for the white women, no use talking about them. For a long time they were considered precious objects, and were feared and respected like fetishes. Now they had come down a few pegs. Now it was known that they were just as easy as the black women, and more venal, and had vices the black women were innocent of. . . . But what was the use of talking about it?

And the white women wished to be respected!

Batouala's father held out his hand. The uproar subsided as if by magic. Not so the sound of music and singing that filled the air.

"My children, everything you say is so. Only, you should see there's nothing to be done. Resign yourselves. When the bamara (lion) roars, the antelope fears to bell. You are not the stronger. Keep quiet.

"Besides, to be quite frank, we are not here to curse the boundjous.

"I am old. While you were discussing, my tongue got dry. Let us shout less and drink more. Next to the bed and the easy-chair, Pernod is the most important invention of the boundjous. My eyesight is not so good, but I thought I noticed several bottles of absinthe. Do you mean to brood on them, Batouala?"

The tension relaxed. They went into fits of laughter. Batouala himself had tears of laughter in his eyes as he hastened to satisfy the waggish old man's desire.

CHAPTER V

THERE was a great commotion.
The huge distant noise had descended on Grimari. Now it
came from somewhere near the crossing of
the roads from Pouyamba and Panka-
goura. It approached nearer and nearer,
it reached the commandant's cattle shed,
it crossed the bridge spanning the Bembe,
and then suddenly it clapped down upon
the Government grounds.

But no longer a huge distant noise.
N'Gakoura had changed it into a band
of young men and women, who advanced
dancing, naked, wild-eyed, their hair
close-shorn, their bodies whitened with
ashes and manioc. '(Death strike him who
did not notice this costume!)

They accompanied their leaps and
bounds with words, nasal or guttural, that

[93]

no one understood. For they used the Samali, the sacred language. They moved under a sort of frenzy regulated by the songs and the koundes.

The crowd on the grounds could now distinguish them.

Shouts went up, an inextinguishable roar, which awoke the hornbills along the Bembe and the Pombo and set them cackling in the moonlit night.

A strange, sudden joy shook the multitude on the grounds. They started to their feet, the warriors seized their weapons, dogs barked, babies wailed, and the women, drunk with kéné, drunk with the tumult, beat their feet on the ground, and shouted, shouted:

"Ga-nza . . . ga-nza . . . ga-nza

The li'nghas set up their hollow booming.

What magic of light upon the land! Only the trees and the leaves seemed the blacker for the scattering of whiteness. The ground was white. The kagas were white. The roads were roads of white linen. The Pombo and the Bembe rolled waters of moonlight.

The warriors waited crouching behind their shields, their javelins in their fists.

At a roll of the tom-toms they raised themselves upright, and with lifted shields and brandished javelins, rushed down to the Bembe. There, swiftly turning, they ran back to their starting point with loud outcries.

The ga'nzas danced to their place. An overwhelming burst of shouts, songs, balafons, koundes, li'nghas.

The festivity now began in full form. The leaders were the moukoundjis-yangba. See how they had consecrated themselves—with long birds' feathers in their plaited hair and bells tinkling at wrists, knees and ankles.

Three of them, swinging their arms and knocking their knees together, came forward to perform mummeries. Their grimaces increased the crowd's delight.

By degrees the emotions of the crowd spread and swelled into a frenzy. The ringing of the bells on the mokoundjis-yangba sounded louder and louder amid the clapping of hands and the smacking of tongues. The dance, the dance! Now for the dance!

A tremor went through the crowd.

Children came forward into the space left clear by the throngs surrounding the ga'nzas, and danced.

They gesticulated, they shook their bodies, they waved their arms and legs, and went through extravagant contortions, unconsciously imitating the adults they had seen dancing in the moonlight outside the huts.

Women came to take their places, stepping single file, the one behind with her hands on the shoulders of the one in front. They were naked, their hair was anointed with castor-oil, their ears, lips and nostrils were hung with vari-colored glass beads, copper bracelets encircled their wrists and ankles.

They formed a large round, and began to move and turn like fire-flies in the dusk.

At a signal from a tom-tom the round opened into a semicircle.

With a rhythmic chant and the regular beat of their hands and feet, the women sustained the cadence of the koundes, li'nghas and balafons.

Faster went the tempo.

One of the women dancers, covered with perspiration, her eyes closed, her body slack, moved to the middle and front of the semicircle made by the parted round. Should she show signs of falling, there would be those behind to catch her, and those at the horns of the crescent to keep her upright.

She took three steps forward—hand-clapping in regular beats—one, two, three. She offered herself to an invisible someone. Rebuffed! She recoiled—one, two, three.

As if overcome by weakness and shame at continued rejection, she let herself fall backward. Her friends ran to support her. In despair she moved, according to the rules of the dance, to the left tip of the figure, while one of the women at the opposite tip moved to the centre, to try in her turn for success where the other had failed.

When the time came for the men—delirium! Mouths wide-open in deafening shouts, faces dissolved in sweat, a beating and a stamping that shook the ground.

And what cries! What laughter! What gestures! For the presence of so many men and women, the beer, the hemp, the dancing, the joy, had redoubled the thrilling warmth of desire.

There were twelve men, almost naked.

Bissibingui was the handsomest of all. The strongest too. His muscles stood out, his eyes glowed like the brush on fire. He commanded his companions because he dominated them with his fine, tall, vigorous, sinewy figure.

Their bodies were smeared red with oil and powdered cam-wood, and hung with bells and grelots from feathered head-gear down to the cords tying their loin cloths.

A strong smell came from their skin. The sweat of fatigue rolled over their tattooing. Fatigue! They were not aware of it. All they cared about was the yangba.

Life was short. The day soon came when one was unfit, even for love. Did not every sun bring death nearer? Ah, what better than to enjoy life while there was still time!

They danced.

They bent low, touched the ground with their hands, and held them there long enough for two or three antics. Then they suddenly threw them back and, with their bodies still bent, stamped their feet alternately while waving their arms, up and down, up and down, like the wings of a great kite that has pounced upon its prey, has caught it in its claws, and indolently volplanes in the motionless sky.

Finally they wheeled about, made a tremendous leap, landing on hands and feet, and matched their gestures to the tom-tom of the li'nghas.

> Ga'nza . . . ga'nza .   ga'nza!
> They will give you ga'nza,
> Ga'nza . . . ga'nza . . . ga'nza!

An old man, covered with gris-gris (fetishes) and carrying a knife, stood up in front of the youths. An old woman likewise waited beside the girls. And the elders, close beside the two old people, laughed to see the young people dance, these young ones who were soon to suffer.

> Ga'nza . . . ga'nza . . . ga'nza!
> Girls, you will be women,
> Youths, you will be men,
> This evening after ga'nza,

Ga'nza .   ga'nza   ga'nza!
G. nza .   ga'nza   ga'nza!

The two old people spoke:

"For one moon, for two moons, you have concealed yourselves in the depths of the woods. You have fasted and afflicted yourselves.

"For one moon and another moon you have hidden yourselves away from profane eyes, you have whitened your bodies so that death shall not carry them off to his village.

"You have spoken the sacred language and none other. You have lived off roots and herbs, far from the eyes of the profane.

"For one moon and another moon you have slept no matter where—no matter where and no matter how. You have abstained from laughter and from joy.

"N'Gakoura is well content with you. Your trial is over. You may enjoy yourselves. You may laugh, dance, live in the open, speak, and sleep on your bogbos.

[101]

"You will soon be men. You will soon be women. In a little while you will undergo ga'nza.

"Your trial is over. You may enjoy yourselves. You may laugh and dance."

Ga'nza   ga'nza   ga'nza . . . ga'nza!
Ga'nza   ga'nza   ga'nza . . . ga'nza!

The balafons, li'nghas and koundes thundered like a storm—to stifle possible outcries.

The ceremony began.

The first patient staggered. With cudgels raised in the air, the men rushed upon him. If a trifling pain was enough to upset him, then he was unworthy of being a man. He must be struck down. He must die. That was the will of custom.

But cheating them of their murderous lust, the new ga'nza joined the surrounding crowd. He must pretend to ignore his pain, he must dance and sing.

Ga'nza . . . ga'nza . . . ga'nza .   ga'nza!
A man is ga'nza once in his life.

Indifferent to the uproar, the two old

people went about their business, mechanically, hearing nothing, seeing nothing.
They resembled reapers at harvest-time
who go through the fields carrying sickles.

Young girls, very pale, certain of what
was coming, danced in gyrations. In
spite of everything they could not help
trembling with fear.

The old woman came up and attended
to the girls.

Ga'nza . . . ga'nza   ga'nza   ga'nza!
A man is ga'nza, a woman, too,
But once in life.
You are one of us now, men!
You are one of us, women!
Now you are ga'nzas.
Ga'nza . . . ga'nza . . . ga'nza   ga'nza!

The ceremony was over.

The tumult reached its height.

What had gone before was nothing.
All the preceding noises and outcries, the
confused dancing had only been a preparation for what was to come—the dance
of love, scarcely ever danced but on this

evening, when they were permitted to indulge in debauchery and crime.

The li'nghas, the balafons, the koundes vied with each other in a frenzy.

The hornbills, awakened out of their sleep, cackled grimly. The night birds of prey made a frightened fuss over the yangba. But their hooting was drowned in this explosion of madness.

Two women appeared. One of them was Yassiguindjia, the wife of Batouala, the mokoundji. The other was still a virgin.

They were naked. They wore necklaces of glass beads, rings in their ears and noses, and jingling bracelets round their wrists and ankles. Their bodies were overlaid with a dark red glaze.

In addition to these festive adornments, Yassiguindjia wore an emblem that indicated the rôle she was to play in the dance.

At first she danced only with her hips. Her feet never moved from the one spot.

Then, slowly, she glided rather than walked up to her partner.

The girl drew back. She did not want to yield. Her face and gestures expressed alarm. Yassiguindjia, feigning disappointment, stepped backward and stamped violently. The girl, having recovered from her unreasonable alarm, offered herself from a distance. The woman glided up to her again. The girl suffered her to come closer.

Thus the dance of love continued to the end, the girl resisting, the man, symbolized in Yassiguindjia, trying to win her love, and finally succeeding.

A strange madness shook the human welter surrounding the dancers.

A smell of sweat and alcohol spread, more pungent than the smoke.

Couples formed. They danced as Yassiguindjia and her friend had danced.

Intoxication. It was the immense joy of brutes loosed from all control.

They came to words and blows. Blood

flowed. No difference. Desire alone was master.

More of the tom-tom, but no more of the kounde or balafon. The performers wanted to share in the joy they had evoked, maintained, and increased.

They mingled with the crowd and danced the dance of love, the chief dance, the one from which all the others derive without ever equalling it.

They danced.

A warm vapor arose from the multitude like the mists that steam up from the earth after rain.

A couple, dancing, fell to the ground.

Suddenly, his fingers twitching about a knife in his hand, Batouala the mokoundji rushed upon this couple.

He was foaming. His fist was raised for the blow.

More nimbly than n'gouhilles (monkeys) Bissibingui and Yassiguindjia leapt out of his reach. He pursued them.

Ah, those children of a dog had the

impudence to desire each other before his very eyes!

He'd have the skin of that strumpet. As for Bissibingui, he'd castrate him. Ah, wouldn't the women make fun of him then!

Yassiguindjia! The idea! Hadn't he bought her with seven waist-cloths, a box of salt, three copper collars, a bitch, four pots, six hens, twenty she-goats, forty big baskets of millet, and a girl slave!

Ah, he'd make Yassiguindjia take the test poison.

The outcries and the unspeakable confusion were succeeded by a swiftly-descending, tremendous stupor.

Then, all of a sudden, in the silence, a shout went up.

"The commandant! The commandant!"

There was a general stampede for the villages.

"The commandant! The commandant!"

Gradually the multifarious noise of the fleeing horde passed into silence.

Amid the debris of all sorts, the food and the fires, only one old man remained. Leaning against one of the li'nghas, he seemed to be sound asleep.

One—two! One—two! One—two! Right about face! Att——"

The thump of the butt-ends of muskets upon the ground. The tourougous had returned.

"Ixe!" Sergeant Sillatigui Kotnaté shouted in command. Then, in a moment or two: "Po!"

The commandant arrived on horseback at a gentle trot.

"Right-dress!" the sergeant commanded again.

"What does this mess mean, Sandoukou?" asked the commandant, calling the sergeant by his native nickname. "And what was the rumpus I heard only a moment ago?"

"Your honor, Boula is a simpleton and a lazybones. The M'bis and their friends felt like coming here and getting drunk.

The men I met on the road a little while ago told me so."

"Good. Excellent. This very day the M'bi chiefs shall pay me one hundred francs fine. If not let them beware of prison—a whipping first, then prison."

"Very well, your honor."

"And who is that dirty nigger asleep over there?"

"That—that is the father of Batouala."

"What's he doing there, the drunken beast?"

"I think he's passed out. Too much kéné. You don't see any bottles of Pernod beside him?"

"One dirty beast the less. No matter. Batouala must come right away and remove his old father's carcass double quick. —And that noodle Boula. Where is he— that three-legged calf, that dolt, that ninny? Ah, there he is. How do you do, Kouloungoulou! How do you do, my dear sir. Get out of here with your dirty mug. I don't know what keeps me from

smashing in that big, flat nose of yours.
I will some day. In the meanwhile, to
teach you how to take care of the grounds
while I am away, will you permit me to
give you two weeks in prison, one week
without pay. And now off with you—
out of here as fast as you can, you piece of
dung. I flatter you by calling you that.
Mr. Boula is displeased? Yes? If so, all
Mr. Boula need do is run to the Governor
and complain. And the Governor, if he's
in as much of a hurry as am I to pester
him—! Sillattigui, everybody is to keep
quiet—today—Sunday. Understand? . . .
Dismissed!"

A heavy mist had crept upon the country. The frogs croaked.

It was dawn, the dawn of a day in the
dry season.

CHAPTER VI

EVERY day is not a holiday. After the dry season comes the rainy season, songs of mourning follow songs of joy, tears follow laughter.

In full yangba the father of Batouala had crossed the black brush for the far-away village whence no one has ever returned.

To die while drinking! There is no sweeter death. Intoxication deadens the pangs of consciousness To die while drinking is only to slip from sleep to death. No anguish, no suffering. It is a gliding, a steady, infinite gliding down into shadow. No thought, no resistance.

What a delight!

And then—nothing more, nothing more. You go to rest somewhere in the country of N'Gakoura, unless you go to the country of Kolikongbo.

No mosquitoes, no fog, no cold, no work. No taxes to pay or sandoukous to lug. Ill-treatment, oaths of fealty to foreign masters, lashings? Nini! Mata! Absolute serenity, endless peace. No bother, no desires. Everything in abundance, and for nothing—even women.

Since the boundjous had come, the poor dear blacks had only one refuge left, death. Death alone delivered them from bondage. Happiness was nowhere to be found except over yonder, in those dark distant regions from which the whites were formally excluded.

For eight days and eight sleeps women mourners and chanters around the corpse of Batouala's father, which was lashed to a tree, had sent up their lamentations. In sign of mourning they had dusted their hair with ashes and blackened their faces with charcoal. They cried and danced, they tore their breasts and limbs.

The others present mumbled the funeral songs.

> Baba (father), thou alone art happy.
> We, who mourn thee,
> We have need of pity.

Ah, but for the dictates of custom there would have been no life in their wearied monotone!

After all a dead man was not interesting. What was there to expect of him? Being beyond recall he had lost all value. He no longer belonged to the community. He was as useless to the tribe as a dried leaf or a gnawed bone.

Only custom and the elders demanded that dancing, to the rhythm of doleful songs, should accompany him who traversed invisible paths to the village of N'Gakoura or Kolikongbo, which was so remote that no one who went there ever returned.

He was dead, he surely was, the father of Batouala. No doubt of it. After a week's exposure, and seeing that swarms of big green voumas (flies) greedily attacked his decaying body, it was high time to "plant" him in the ground.

> Baba, thou alone art happy.
> We, who mourn thee,
> We have need of pity.

Besides, the chase was in full swing.

Every evening the dense smoke that mounted from the whole horizon straight up to the sky announced glorious doings in the fine mornings to follow. Every evening when the tom-toms sounded, the breeze brought the flying bits of burnt vegetation and the fragrance of scented plants. It was the season that invited to the beating for game.

Custom having been duly observed, the bothersome corpse had better be "planted" in the ground as quickly as possible.

Custom! Nowadays very little heed was paid to custom. The young people and all, generally speaking, who served with the whites turned away from custom in ridicule.

Out of ignorance youth was wilfully mocking. It jeered at old men and their wisdom. It made no effort to reason. Or rather, it thought that a laugh was as good as a reason.

But custom was the entire experience of the elders, and the elders of the elders. Into it they piled all their knowledge as rubber is piled into a basket.

So it was not for nothing that custom required a full week's exposure of a corpse, and even more.

That week of exposure, which the whites considered silly, was justified on two good accounts. For one thing it gave the entire family time to be present at the funeral.

M'bis departed, one after another, without cease—like all the Negroes for that matter. An M'bi was here to-day, gone to-morrow. The day after, no trace of him was left.

So, quickly, the tom-tom spoke. Its summons was received and transmitted. Its call leapt from valley to valley, crossed the kagas, rumbled in the undergrowth, passed on, rolled from lake to lake, from village to village bringing each and every-one the fatal news. And he who was inter-ested, for whom the summons was meant, hurried to go where it was his duty to go.

That was one of the reasons, in fact the main reason, for the long exposure of the bodies of the dead.

There was another reason. The elders of the elders had observed that sometimes a man thought to be dead was not dead: corpses had come back to life. From which the elders had deduced that one could sleep for several days as the dead slept and yet be alive.

Now dare to say that long exposure of the bodies of the dead was wrong.

The body of one who had actually de-parted for the distant country did not take long to fall into decay. Its very stench spoke, in place of the language of the living, and told of its desire to be buried.

Do you suppose the whites could translate this mute language and admit the wisdom of custom!

Such were the thoughts of Batouala. In a low voice he confided them to Bissibingui.

The two were seated side by side at the funeral ceremony. They had become reconciled the morning after the festival of the ga'nzas and seemed to be as close friends as ever. Bissibingui's voluptuousness and Batouala's violence were charged to the account of intoxication.

But Bissibingui knew that Batouala plotted revenge, and Batouala knew that Bissibingui knew.

> Baba, thou alone art happy.
> We, who mourn thee,
> We have need of pity.

A white man saw red the moment something angered him.

Bandas or Mandjias, Sangos or Goubous proceeded differently. Revenge was not a food to be eaten hot. Hate might well be concealed under a guise of affection; friendliness being the ashes that were spread upon the fire of hate to keep it smouldering.

Huts, planted fields, goats, even money were all placed at the enemy's disposal. All. You even tried to anticipate what he might ask for. You had to put his distrust to sleep. You gave him goats of a pure white or yellow, and hens of a pure white or yellow, the color of these matabich (presents) symbolizing friendship stainless and indestructible.

The game of deception might be kept up a long time. It was simply a question of knowing how to bide your time. To hate meant to have infinite patience.

Then the right day would come, the occasion would seem favorable: you poisoned the man who had once been your more than brother, your ouandja. You poisoned him, or else you killed him by "making the panther."

Aha! Aha! Making the panther? One more thing the whites knew nothing about. Ee-hee!

That was the manner of death Batouala had selected for his excellent ouandja, Bissibingui.

Mourou, the panther, was the cruel beast who roamed the brush, especially on moonless nights.

With fang and claw he slowly ripped his victim open, and tore it to pieces. With his moustachioed muzzle he smelled the blood before drinking it, the blood that reeked, the blood he loved so. He wallowed in it, made himself drunk with it. And after he had gorged himself, he hunted around, long, long, licking his chops, sniffing the strong odor.

If you imitated mourou, what you did was to hide yourself on a black night in the brush bordering the path along which your ouandja was going to come. You wore a mask and waited.

There! A mighty leap. You had him on the ground. You choked him to death. Then with a jagged knife, or a sharp stone, or your nails, you slit open the veins of his neck, as the panther did; you tore him limb from limb, as the panther did.

Such were Batouala's reflections. Bissibingui reasoned pretty much the same way. Aha! What a wonderful sight was the corpse of an old enemy!

> Baba, thou alone art happy.
> We, who mourn thee,
> We have need of pity.

A child was playing with that strange lizard, the koli'ngo. Everybody knew that the koli'ngo, according to the place it was in, turned black, green, yellow, or red.

But did Djouma the little yellow dog with pointed ears—did he know it? No. He couldn't know it. That was why he barked himself hoarse at the koli'ngo, while that skeleton of a Kosseyende, gone crazy from the sleeping-sickness, imitated, like the fool he was, the wailing of the mourners, the cries of the child playing with the koli'ngo, the barking of Djouma, and the chanting of the women chanters.

Batouala made a sign and rose.

Captive slaves laid the slight body on one of the mats the dead man had used while alive.

The dull roll of the li'nghas mingled with the wailing chant of the mourners.

> We shall take you now,
> O father of Batouala,
> To your new abode.
>
> Have no regrets for life.
> In the land of Kolikongbo
> Happier you'll be than we.
>
> You will eat and drink
> Till hunger and thirst are gone.
> No need for more.

After the final preparations had been

made, they went to the spot where they were going to "plant" the remains of him who had been a man. The place selected was a little way from the last hut he had lived in.

Two round pits in the ground connected by a subterranean gallery. That was the grave.

A woman slave slid down the one pit, the corpse was let down the other The slave, from the underground gallery, pulled the legs of him whose spirit was travelling to the country of Kolikongbo until they lay straightened out in the gallery.

And now with his back to the side of the pit the father of Batouala sat at rest. He slept sitting. And what an inexhaustible sleep!

The pit to which his legs reached was filled with wood, then with earth.

He felt nothing of this strange damp weight He slept. Wood was heaped upon his passive head. He was conscious of nothing. His eyes did not even open.

A mat was spread over the dry wood, and over the mat earth was heaped. Then they stamped the earth down, they stamped and stamped.

What cared he? He slept. Really, when he slept such a sleep there was no need to lay his clothes out on the trampled ground, and his pots on top of his clothes, and his easy-chair and garabos. There was no need to prepare what he might want for living the life of the dead.

The dry wood and the mat would prevent the earth from falling in and disturbing his sleep. On the other hand he had within reach his ordinary pots and waistcloths, so that if—supposing if—he itched to rise at night and, though dead, wandered about in the villages of the living, and got cold and hungry and thirsty, then he could cook himself something to eat, he could drink, and put on clothes.

But that was improbable. He slept such a sound sleep.

You are in the land of Kolikongbo
Among the elders of the elders.
Some day we will join you there.

Over. It was all over.

They danced about the pits. Then they built a large fire and burned all the dead man's possessions.

You are in the land of Kolikongbo
Among the elders of the elders.
Some day we will join you there.

Night fell, and brought the cold with it.

On the road to Pouyamba was heard, as every evening, the roar of his lordship the lion. The glow-worms lit up the darkness with their tiny torches. Above the fires that warmed the sleep of Batouala and his family hovered the ephemerals born at night.

Days passed.

The roof was removed from the dead man's hut, and the wooden symbol of manhood was broken, the symbol attached to the front of the dwelling of the man who had been the father of a family.

But no one thought of the dead man any more. There were other, more urgent preoccupations.

For one thing it was imperative to find out who had cast the evil eye and caused the disappearance of Batouala's father. We were born to live. If a person died, that was because someone or other had made a yorro, or pronounced incantations. This witchcraft worker had to be discovered.

And after that, ah! after that!

The season of the chase!

Ey-ha! The be'ngue (wart-hog) and his red brother, the solitary voungba (wild boar), were going to fight it out with the dogs.

Ey-ha! How the maddened buffalos would bellow as they rushed pellmell, their tails stretched straight out behind them, their eyes blinded by the smoking and crackling of the flames.

Ah, the small game they would collect in the meshes of their nets! Hares, antelopes, cane-rats. The blood would spurt! Chops and haunches would foam and lather. The red play of the javelins, spears, throwing knives, arrows, would go faster and faster.

And the barking of the dogs, oh, the barking of the dogs as they hung on to the flanks of the dying beast!

Was any dead man, no matter how great, worth the joy of movement, the delight of action, the intoxication of slaughter? Was he worth any of the things which are the reason for living?

CHAPTER VII

THE sun was descending toward his hut at the ends of the invisible earth.

He was a kind old man, the sun was, and so just, so impartial. He shone for all living creatures, from the highest to the lowest. He knew neither rich nor poor, neither blacks nor whites. Whatever their lot in life, whatever their color, all men were his children. He loved them equally well. He shone benignantly upon their fields, dispelled the sneaking cold fogs, reabsorbed the rain, drove out the dark.

Ah, the dark. No matter where the dark lodged, the sun pursued it pitilessly. The dark was the one thing he hated. He sent his rays to comfort the ill with their warmest caresses. His light was health, joy, gaiety. Yes, the sun, the good young old man, stood for gaiety, immense, serene, extending its welcome to life.

He could regulate and succeed in accomplishing what man could not regulate or succeed in accomplishing.

Since endless rainy seasons men had followed men like the flowing water in a river. They had children, who in their turn would have children.

The grass which ate the earth, the animals who ate the grass, man who destroyed both grass and animals, all died. Where there had been huts, smoke, life, cattle, fields, villages, there would be the brush. And some day the wild brush, too, would be gone. The rivers would dry up. Vain was man's belief that he survived in the children of his children. The oldest families would be extinguished like fires by rain.

Lolo, however, the good old man, who feared none but Ipeu the moon—since he fled the moon at nightfall—the mokoundji of the gods of heaven and earth, he who was always young and bright, *he* would shine eternally, as he had shone of old, as he shone to-day, as he would shine to-morrow: he would shine when the worlds had disappeared.

On one of the highest rocks of the kaga Kossegamba, Bissibingui lay prone, waiting.

Every now and then his mouth opened in a yawn, the way a kokorro (serpent), coiled round a branch, will open its jaws and show its venomous fangs as if to bite or swallow the sun. Bissibingui yawned, shifted his position, and lay still again.

That little yellow fleck down there, that bare, yellow, shining fleck, was the Government post of the Bembe; it was Grimari.

And from the tiny, tiny house, on an elevation at the end of the bare, yellow, shining fleck, issued the orders to which—strange as it might seem—the M'bis,

Dacpas, Mandjias and Langbassis had whether or no to submit.

Bissibingui's eyes could follow the meanderings of the Bembe by its dark margins of trees which, slowly widening, insinuated themselves between the treeless kagas.

The gendarmes were marching. The noise they made frightened the cibissis (cane-rats), animals with something of the characteristics of both a hare and a rat. The soldiers' feet struck against the stones; dust rose. They marched along, bayonets to shoulders, singing.

A descent. Down to the Dela which flowed into the Bembe. No matter. On they went.

On and on. Kossegamba was now out of their sight. They passed the village of Yabada and the heights of kaga Makala.

Few undulations in the country now, but huts everywhere. The land of the Langbassis, the villages of Lissa.

Planted fields everywhere. Plains

everywhere, plains, plains, plains. At
the end of the plains the Deka which emp-
tied into the Kandjia. For in the mean-
time the Bembe—N'Gakoura alone knows
how—had changed into the Kandjia.

Beyond, more tribes, which Bissibingui
no longer knew. Beyond, also, the Niou-
bangui, the broad river, the mother of all
rivers, on which the whites in the season
of the high waters steered, as far as Mo-
baye, giant canoes that went without oars
and spat smoke from the tube of a sort of
fat pipe.

Bissibingui had visited those parts.
They were all rich in wild cattle, and were
interesting, therefore, as hunting-grounds.

But it was better to let the gogouas
(wild cattle, buffalos) stay where they
were than have dealings with a Dacpa,
the vilest, the most treacherous of men—
the whites excepted.

A great boredom went up from the
deadly stillness of the brush. The heat

fell upon it like metals in fusion poured into a smith's bapana.

A musket shot rang out followed by smoke blacker than the smoke that crowned the flight of the kites.

For two months daily, from sunrise to sunset, fire had been set to grass and thicket. For two months the dark had been lit up by the flare of the conflagrations.

And the wind whipped up the flames; the wind carried afar the echo of the dry crackling of the flames.

Bissibingui was waiting.

On the path winding about the flank of Kossegamba a woman appeared.

She advanced leisurely, a pipe in her mouth, her hand up to her head balancing a calabash.

Bissibingui recognized her immediately: it was Yassiguindjia, prompt for the appointment which he had found the opportunity to arrange with her the previous day.

They shook hands in silence and seated themselves side by side.

No need to hide. For the present they had nothing to fear. Everybody was engaged in the chase. The most populous villages were deserted, save for the old men, the sick, those whose eyes were dead, women in labor, goats and chickens.

As for the dogs, all the Djoumas of all the villages had left with their masters.

Bissibingui admired Yassiguindjia.

How he desired her! The very sunlight itself seemed to stream through his limbs along the blue veins in which his blood circulated.

A red cord bound her forehead, around her throat was a three-stringed necklace of shells, and around her ankles heavy rings of red copper. She was charming. A small bit of wood pierced the lobe of her left ear, another bit of wood her right nostril. These ornaments gave her an air of distinction especially becoming to her.

She had flat breasts, large hips, strong round limbs, and dainty ankles.

She, too, was studying her companion, surreptitiously.

Bissingbui enjoyed that strength in suppleness which is the beauty of males.

His frame was perfect, his shoulders and chest fairly snapped with muscles. His abdomen was flat, his legs long, rounded and sinewy. He was so fleet of foot he could probably outstrip the trumpeting elephant. And didn't Yassiguindia know how virile he was? Didn't the women who had once had him try to keep him by might and main? Didn't they descend to pleading and tears? Didn't they submit to his insults, his brutalities, his scorn?

"Bissibingui," she said, "I must look out. I must be more careful than ever. The sorcerer declared it was my fault that Batouala's father died; he said I sent him an evil spirit. Protect me, Bissibingui. Protect me. You are strong. If you do not put yourself between them and me, they will kill me. The incantations have already begun. So far they have turned out favorable to me. The other day in my presence they bled a black hen. Just before she died they left her to herself, and she fell to the left, not to the right. You know what that meant—that Yassiguindjia was not guilty, and they should look for someone else who had cast the evil spell. But they consulted the elders, and the elders would not admit the evidence of this sign. So, I must wait to take the test poisons. To be sure I'm not afraid of all the poisons. Gou'ndi, for instance, doesn't hurt me a bit. I can even drink a lot of it. That's the only way to make it harmless. But even if I'm safe from poison, how can I avoid the other dangers? You may rest assured my tormentors won't wish to atone for their lies by giving me the presents that custom requires in this case. What! give me two women, two slaves! Never! They'd pre-

fer to throw latcha in my eyes. And my
eyes would die, because I don't know the
antidote for latcha. Then they'd all shout
that N'Gakoura had spoken, that my dead
eyes were proof of my guilt. They'd beat
me, they'd stone me. All the dogs who
hate me because I used to repulse them
would take advantage of my weakness.
Bissibingui, Bissibingui, they will want
me to plunge my hands into boiling water.
They will put a red-hot iron to my loins.
Bissibingui, Bissibingui, I shall have to
undergo the tortures of hunger and thirst.
I shall be cold! And then, while I'm still
alive, they will bury me beside Batouala's
father, to appease his anger by my death.
Bissibingui, I want you! You know I
want you—you, only you! Is it my fault
if we haven't been able to belong to each
other yet? I am being watched jealously.
You too. You are being watched jealously. I shouldn't be surprised if someone was spying on us at this moment.
But there's no use raising dam on dam,

you see: water always seeks water. Even
the kagas, big as they are, cannot prevent
two rivers from joining. So, if you want
me anything like the way I want you, I'll
be yours in a few days, no one but yours.
—Make up your mind."

The sun was no longer so hot. The
tom-toms and the oliphants were sending
out invitations. They told Bissibingui
that Batouala was expecting him, that until he arrived Batouala would not set fire
to the brush of the hunting courses that
lay between the Dacpa village of Soumana and the N'Gapu village of Yakidji.

Yassiguindjia continued:

"You're angry at me to-day, aren't you,
Bissibingui? But you know I want you
more than you can want me. All of me
wants you. I belong to you. You told
me to come; I came. But I cannot be
yours here. Let us run away. Then I
will be yours. I will cook for you, wash
your clothes, sweep your hut, sow your
fields and weed them. All these things I

will do if only you and I will go away from here together. Will you? We'll go to Bangui, where you can enter service as a tourougou. Once a tourougou, what M'bi would dare to complain against you? Not one—not even Batouala.

"There's a good reason, you see, why the commandants understand nothing but what their tourougous want them to understand. Let us go. I don't want to take poison through my mouth. I don't want to plunge my hands in boiling water. I don't want my eyes to die. I don't want to die. I am young, healthy, strong, I can still live many seasons of rains. And to live is to be with the man one wants."

Bissibingui got up and stretched himself.

The canoe of the sun, full of blood, was darkening on the horizon.

The carolling of the birds had ceased. Silence spread, the same silence as preceded the sunrise in the morning.

"Yassiguindjia, what you have said is right. I must think it over. But I swear to you, by N'Gakoura, that you will be safe. This is not the time to run away. Wait until the chase is over. Then I'll go to Bangui to enter the service. A tourougou carries a musket, cartridges, and a big knife fastened on the left side to a leather belt. He is well dressed, he wears a chechia and sandals, and he receives pay. And every Sunday when the tatalita— (euphonic for the blowing of a horn) has sounded "Dismissed," he can go make his little pe'ndere in the villages, where the women admire him. And this is not all. There are other advantages, besides. Instead of paying taxes we tourougous help to collect them—by pillaging the villages; both the villages that still have the taxes to pay and those that have already paid. We make the villagers pound the rubber; we gather in the recruits for carrying the sandoukous. That's what a tourougou has to do. Wherever we go the chiefs and

their men, to secure our good will, heap
us with presents. These little privileges
make the life of a tourougou pleasant,
easy, enjoyable, especially as the commandants don't know the language of the
country well—our country, our language.
So supposing a certain village hasn't been
very generous with gifts. What do we
do? We invent one of those delightful
stories which have neither head nor tail,
and we tell it to the excellent commandant.
He, always being a just, sensible, clear-
sighted man, begins by imprisoning the
entire population—chickens, chiefs, children, dogs, women, goats, slaves, crops.
Then the chickens, goats, dogs, crops and
women are sometimes auctioned off, and
the money so obtained swells the taxes.
Occasionally the goats and chickens are
distributed among friends, that is, if they
are not presented to the Governor, who
will remember the courtesy when the time
comes for promotions. In the latter case
we tourougous are allowed to share in the

dogs, women, and crops. To be sure, it
is only the peaceful commandants who use
these deplorable methods Fortunately
the commandants are not all alike. Else
where should we blacks be, N'Gakoura?
There are warlike commandants, too;
more of them, in fact, than of the other
kind. They bestride a fiery steed which
never runs out of a gentle trot. The boys
and the boys of the boys follow. So they
start off to war against the poor wretches
who have reached the end of their resistance. When the expedition is over, the
commandants send piles of betis to the
Government telling of their prowess and
ours. A lie doesn't weigh heavy on the
commandants. And everybody's happy:
we for making fun of them, they for having told a splendid story woven out of
their pure imagination. . . . But now I
must go, Yassiguindjia. I am being summoned on all sides. I must go. Wherever you walk may the way be a pleasant
one, Yassiguindjia."

"Wherever you walk may the way be a pleasant one, Bissibingui."

She followed him with her eyes. His figure grew smaller and smaller. He disappeared.

She balanced the calabash of viands on her head, and, in her turn, went slowly on her way.

A soft starry dusk had spread. The fragrance of scented plants floated in the air. The dusk made a frame round the ruddy glow of the brush fires.

In the heavens hung the moon, curved like a throwing knife, delicately luminous. A brilliant star shone in a great dark-blue empty space.

Blessed peace, tranquil lights, life in which, it seemed, nothing dreadful could ever happen, beauty of living—complete and perfect save for the broken silence.

For the roll of the tom-toms, blurred by contrary winds or muffled by the distance, boomed out in the night.

CHAPTER VIII

BISSIBINGUI walked through the night.

He carried a torch in his right hand, and was armed with a bow, a quiver of arrows, and a huge likongo (spear) of thick, heavy iron, instead of the usual javelin. In addition to these he had two throwing knives with him, an ample wallet filled with viands, and a dagger strapped under his left forearm.

Thus he walked through the endless night, calm, unhurried, but with eyes alert and ears pricked for the faintest sound. How long had he been walking? He did not know. Only the boundjous were able to divide time into equal parts. These parts they shut up in a little box with two, sometimes three needles of unequal length and rapidity that moved nimbly on top of certain figures.

The kaga Kossegamba. The brook Boubou Yabao, the delicious bath he had had in the Boubou. The little village nearby built by one of the head-men of the chief Delepou. The road to the Government grounds. The commandant's stables a javelin's throw from the Bembe, and next to them the cemetery where the whites buried their dead. The Bembe, then the big bridge that spanned the Bembe. Finally the Government grounds, the planted fields, the commandant's kitchen garden, the great shed which always sheltered the chiefs and their men when they came to market rubber.

After crossing the Pombo, Bissibingui skirted Batouala's village and made for one of the desolate huts where dwelt Macoude the fisherman. From him he would learn just where to find Batouala.

Macoude told him, and added, as he took leave, some obscure recommendations, the very haziness of which made Bissibingui's danger clear to him.

To delay longer would be fatal. He must act, and act quickly.

For a second he entertained the idea of ignoring Batoula's invitation and not attending the chase. On second thought it seemed to him his absence might appear strange. What would he risk? Meeting Batouala surrounded by his own people. It was not worth disappointing him.

A fine breeze! It brought the blare of trumpets, the crackling of flames, and the summons of the li'nghas leaping from echo to echo.

He must act quickly, or die. But what should he do and where should he do it?

The weather was fair. Tom-toms. Bats. Owls. Fire-flies. Fires in the distance. A heaven of stars. And dew, ah the dew.

How pleasant it was!

Yes, but—what was he to do? He would not be killed that night, surely not that night. A murder was not committed before witnesses.

Very well. But how was *he*, Bissibingui, to rid himself of Batouala? Hmm, a
little likou'ndou (poison) would do. He
would mix it surreptitiously with Batouala's food and drink. "Making the panther" certainly had its attractions, and the
javelin was not to be scorned. But the
two latter methods left traces. Not so the
likou'ndou.

Bissibingui had thrown his torch away
and was walking by the light of a great
red glow which the wind seemed to lift
in one leap straight up to the sky. He held
his eyes fixed on the ground to avoid roots
and stones, and kept thinking as he
walked.

Near Pouyamba the fire had surrounded a kaga and was scaling it on all
sides, in sudden licks and curls, snatching
at the rocks or encircling some wretched
tree, climbing up, up to the top, never
letting go, not even after the tree had
fallen into the night and lighted up the
dark with its ruins.

How and where to kill Batouala? Await the occasion? No, it wouldn't do to wait. Provoke it? Ah, there was the difficulty.

The final attempt. At the peak of the kaga, the flames united in one huge embrace, and the smoke went up, dense, lurid.

He would kill Batouala, or Batouala would kill him. Certainly to kill was pleasanter than to be killed. When one was young and the women yielded to one's desires, life had charm.

He looked about. Fires everywhere. The kagas flared like torches in the night.

He *must* kill Batouala.

Aha, aha! How about accidents of the chase? They occurred often enough. How about it! One aimed at an animal and killed a man. Not everybody was skilful. And the best marksman might miss his shot. Ey-hey!

And how about the brush fires? Think of the number of wretches who were burned to a crisp every year! The fire devoured everything, not knowing what it did or whither it went. If one merely paused too long at some spot in the hunting course, it came upon one—the fire which respected nothing but water—and that only in a fury of ill-temper—then all was over.

Then brush fire or hunting accident.

He caught his nose.

Ugh! What a stench! There must be people about. No odor was so unpleasant as that left by men. The smell stuck to your nose, and followed and tormented you. What a stench! Ugh! There were surely people about.

Bissibingui peered intently. Every turn of the path in the dark might conceal a lurking enemy. It was well to be prudent and keep a careful look-out.

Ah, an ant-hill. And another ant-hill laid upon it lengthwise. Bissibingui went to the right because the second ant-hill was placed with the cap on the right.

Farther on he noticed a branch broken

off at the height of his shoulder, a bit of
carved wood beneath, and a sprig of brush,
all pointing to the left. He turned to the
left. A narrow path. That was the way.

He followed these signs mechanically.
The boundjous were wrong if they
thought the brush was dead. The brush
talked from morning to night, from night
to morning like an old woman.

The booming of the tom-toms on the
double convexity of the li'nghas, the toot
of the trumpets or of the oliphants, cries
misleadingly like the calls of certain birds,
the signalling by fires from one height to
another, grass laid across the middle of
the road, one ant-hill set on top of another
ant-hill according to an invariable custom, tufts of wattled leaves, two bits of
wood laid crosswise—here was a living language, a rich language, a language of
light, and sound, and silence.

Praised be the brush! They thought
it was dead? The brush was alive, very
alive, and spoke to its children, but only

to its children. It used whatever language it wanted—smoke, sounds, smells, inanimate objects—to address the spaces it commanded, the spaces where the grass and trees grew and the wild cattle roamed.

Praised be the brush, the brush of the kagas and the brush of the swamp, the brush of the forests and the brush of the plains.

Threatening barks. The flicker of a rubber torch. Two drunken voices. It was Batouala, his old mother, and Djouma, the little yellow dog with the very pointed ears.

Bissibingui had arrived.

But how was he to kill Batouala? By accident of the chase or by burning in the brush fire?

At the moment, however, wasn't it more imperative for him to think of self-defense rather than attack? In spite of warnings he had fallen, unsuspecting, into the rude trap that had been laid for him.

CHAPTER IX

BISSIBINGUI instantly realized how imprudent he had been. Every precaution seemed to have been taken. Here were he and this drunken man, who had trapped him like a child, practically alone together in a clearing far from the highways; witnesses there were none.

But yes, there were witnesses, two, Batouala's "mamma" and Djouma, the little yellow dog. As good as no witnesses, though, they were. A mother, unless she is a most unnatural mother, never betrays her child. And Djouma could certainly be counted upon not to make any revelations. Who in man's memory had ever heard a dog talk!

So, keep your eyes open, Bissibingui, my friend, watch close. If not!——

He seated himself at a distance from Batouala, stuck the point of his likongo in the ground, and drew out his dagger. His assailant would have to pay dear.

He refused the food and millet beer his hosts offered him and pretended not to notice their disappointment.

"Macoude has already stuffed me with potatoes, smoked fish and kéné. I don't want any more, Batouala. You think I'm lying. Feel my wallet. It's crammed with things to eat."

Djouma came and licked his hands. He petted the dog, who rolled on the ground in ecstasy, sneezed, wagged his tail, yapped, gnawed playfully at the caressing fingers.

But Djouma was a dog like every other dog, that is, a less than nothing. So Bissibingui stopped fooling with this less than nothing, and threw stones at him while he pondered the situation.

Batouala, who was getting drunker every moment, rose to dance a few figures of the dance of love—so he thought; for all he did was to reel and stagger. His head and limbs were heavy, his eyes red and swollen. He stumbled over a root and fell prone.

Djouma raced round barking. It was great sport for the little dog.

"The same accident happened to Iili'-ngou once upon a time," said Batouala rising to his feet and bursting into a laugh.

"I think I'll tell you the story of Iili' ngou. You probably don't know a word of it, so listen.

"At that time, as in our day, the earth with its brush, its forests, its rivers, its elephants, and panthers was boundless. Men there were already, and so was the cold. But for the cold, the people would have been happy. It was the one thing they complained about: it took the nimbleness from their limbs, it cut short their sleep. Their complaints about the cold were so loud and so long that Ipeu, the moon, finally sent Iili'ngou, whose other name is Selafou, to teach them the use of fire.

"From the dwelling of the moon down to the earth is a long, long way. So to hasten the coming of Iili'ngou, Ipeu let him down by a tremendously long rope with a li'ngha attached to the one end. When Iili'ngou beat tom-tom on the li'ngha, but not before, the rope was to be pulled up again.

"From Iili'ngou men soon learned that fire was meant not only for dispelling the cold, but for warming their bodies, and cooking their food, and lighting up the dark as well. He became their best friend. They questioned him about everything that seemed mysterious to them.

"For instance, they saw that all living creatures disappeared sooner or later; and gradually a great fear assailed their livers. Where went the spirits of these animals who lay down to sleep one day never to rise again? No use talking to them, flattering them, petting them; they remained unresponsive, silent, motionless. The flies crept up their nostrils, their bodies, alas! turned into a vile creeping and crawling of maggots and worms.

"So the people appealed to the knowledge of Iili'ngou. But he had no answer to allay their apprehensions, and he went back to his lord and master, Ipeu, and said:

" 'The race of men is troubled. They are in fear of death, and they beseech me to find out from you if they are subject to the laws that rule the beasts.'

" 'Go quickly and reassure them, Iili'-ngou, my good man. I have made them in my image. I, myself, die, but I die to be born again, eight sleeps after my disappearance. Let them remember this, and that they may have faith in what I say, you Iili'ngou, shall henceforth live among them.'

"Iili'nghou, straddling his li'ngha, slid down the rope again. He held on with both hands, but was reflecting distractedly upon a whole lot of things, and lo! thinking he had reached the earth, he let go of both the rope and the li'ngha and fell into the void. No need to say that he died from the fall.

"Since that time men die, too."

Bissibingui listened to Batouala. Thoughts whirled through his mind. Batouala had unveiled mysteries that were revealed to none but the very old. Uhu! Beware! His, Bissibingui's death, then, had been decided upon. Beware, beware! It was merely a matter now of the occasion. Perhaps even the very next instant.

"You spoke of fire, Batouala? Do you mean to say that Iili'ngou at Ipeu's order descended to earth to teach men? Perhaps so. But the tribes who live on the shores of the Nioubangui think differently. According to them fire was discovered by the ancestor of all the ancestors of Djouma.

"One day the first dog was playing at

scratching up the earth. He had dug a fairly large hole in the ground when all of a sudden he set up a long agonized howl and jumped from one paw to the other paw, whining with pain.

"His master, attracted by the noise and his wild behavior, went over to the hole, stuck his foot in, and iaow! he too was burned. He had discovered fire.

"That's what the Yakoma paddlers told me."

"Your Yakomans are festering boils of falsehoods. I tell you it's from Iili'ngou, and from no one else that men know fire. It was Iili'ngou, too, who made the earth, and piled up the kagas, and marked the descent of the rivers. But it was Ipeu who made the first man and the first woman.

"I know many more things, Bissibingui, many things that it isn't well for you to know, because you are already wiser than a man of your age should be."

Bissibingui ignored the threat: words

were not deeds. He contented himself
with keeping a careful eye upon Batouala's least movements, and he paid no attention to the old woman's chuckling and
cackling.

"Do you know that Ipeu, the moon, is
the enemy of Lolo, the sun?" Batouala
began again. "You don't, do you? Well,
very, very long ago Lolo, who is both a
man and a woman, lived on good terms
with Ipeu. At the time of which I talk,
Ipeu and Lolo each had a mamma, and
they loved their mammas more than words
can tell.

"Ipeu's mamma felt too cold, and
Lolo's mamma felt too hot. So Lolo took
charge of Akera, Ipeu's mamma, while
Ipeu took charge of Lolo's mamma. It
was an unlucky exchange. Akera, accustomed to the cold, died of the heat, and
Lolo's mamma, accustomed to the heat,
died of the cold.

"From then on Lolo and Ipeu hated
each other. And that is why Ipeu hides

from the sun when Lolo shines hot upon
the land, and also why Ipeu, being the
more powerful of the two, forces Lolo to
run away at the gathering of dusk.

"You didn't know this, eh, Bissibingui?
And you didn't know that the amberepi
(stars) shining up there—numberless
ten-cent pieces, or the winking of eyes
upon eyes—are nothing but holes through
which the drops of rain fall down upon
the earth?

"Of old, the women who wanted to be
mothers—and all women of old did want
to be mothers—were not allowed to eat
the meat of goats or tortoises. We knew
then that if they ate goats' meat they
would be struck with sterility, and if they
ate the meat of a tortoise, their children
would be born prematurely old and would
walk as slowly as the tortoise. We know
that our elders could bring down rain at
will. They could, but they never did, except when the time for sowing was at
hand. Then when the sowing-time moon

rode in the heavens, they took handfuls of salt and threw it on a big fire, and the rain came right down, because salt, loving water, has always attracted water.

"We have also been taught that the dondorro is an evil spirit who dwells in our bellies. When you have belly-ache, it is dondorro playing pranks and tormenting you.

"And N'Gakoura, by whom we swear as hard as we can—do you know him? He has a splendid wife, and children more numerous than the grass of the brush. The two oldest, Nadoulou and Nangodjo, help their father rule his villages.

"The family of N'Gakoura cherishes nothing but good will toward men, and generally satisfies our requests, on condition, however, that we bring them all sorts of gifts.

"The sole enemy of the family of N'Gakoura is Kolikongbo. There are only too many signs, alas! of their enmity. We poor wretches inhabiting the earth have always paid for the pots broken in their conflicts: Kolikongbo kills the friends of N'Gakoura, and N'Gakoura kills the friends of Kolikongbo.

"And Dadra (meteor), Dadra, the nimble brother of the stars whom he resembles, Dadra, who on certain fine warm nights may be seen threading his way between heaven and earth before he disappears like a musket shot—do you know who *he* is?

"No, no, no. You couldn't know, and you won't know until you reach the season of white hairs; which I doubt if you ever will. I am one of those who think you won't live to a ripe old age. If a man wants to live for days and days, he had better not love his neighbor's women, and they had better not run after him.

"But then! I prefer to keep quiet. I feel I'm talking more than I should talk. To be sure, it's in your interest. But I'm drunk, and I'm saying things I don't want to say.

"However, before closing my mouth, I'll tell you the legend of Kolikongbo—Trolle is his real name   Kolikongbo is very, very small, so small that he cannot be seen.   Some people go so far as to say that he exists only in the imagination. Nevertheless, he does exist.   He does, it's not a lie.   If he didn't, why would we call a dwarf Kolikongbo?

"Where does he live?   On the heights, in the caves, and inside of wood.   He lives off honey, yams, the fruit of the rubber-tree, and that choicest meat, the meat of the elephant.   If it were not for his small size, he would be like you and me: he has just the same feet and legs and arms and everything else.   One thing though.   Except for the hairs on his head, he hasn't a single hair on his body.   If you were to find a hair, well, I'd be very much surprised.

"Small as he is, Kolikongbo is strong, stronger than all men and all animals taken together.   He's so strong that you'd better not hold out your hand when you meet him: his handshake would tear your fingers off.

"Kolikongbo has immense plantations. He is rich, he is powerful; you can't imagine how rich, how powerful.

"Yet rich as he is, and though his children are as numerous as the human race, it is impossible for him to find enough workers to keep up his vast plantations. In the rainy season nothing will induce him to leave the caves where he rests, but as soon as the fine weather comes, he dons his waist-cloth of leaves and grass, arms himself with a huge likongo (spear), takes up his wallet, the like of which is not to be seen, and starts off for anywhere at all.

"All the roads are good roads to him, all belong to him. He traverses the rocky plateaus where the sun beats down fiercest, and where he does his terrible tricks. He paces up and down, up and down, sweating and blustering.

"In the dry season there are few people on the roads; in the dry season all people are engaged in the chase. Red, bloody meat is far better than all the plantations in the world.

"Ey-hey! Who's there? Someone is coming down Kolikongbo's road. The sun is high in the heavens and hotter than boiling water The man is so tired he doesn't see that Kolikongbo is following in his footsteps, that he has drawn close, that he has jumped on his neck. Ugh! Kolikongbo deals him a blow that would fell an ox. A thousand sparks flash in the victim's eyes, his ears buzz, his throat is dry, he chokes. He throws his arms out and falls. Then he goes to sleep panting like a bellows.

"He sleeps. No time to lose. Quick. Kolikongbo sticks him into the enormous wallet, which is his inseparable companion, and runs to his plantations—quick, quick. There he awakens the sleeper.

" 'Will you work on my plantations?

I will give you plenty to eat. You will have women, boys, chickens, goats. You will not be unhappy, I promise you. But if you accept my proposition, as I hope you will, I warn you: be prepared never to see your village again nor anything that has belonged to you. Do you agree? Answer me.'

"Tempting as is Kolikongbo's offer, his victims generally refuse it. So—ugh!—another blow of a club on the wretch's neck, he is packed up again, and carried back in a few swift bounds to the spot where he was first struck down. When he regains consciousness, his neck hurts, his head is heavy, his legs are limp. His whole body feels bruised and shaken. He tries to recall why. He tries and tries. Kolikongbo, however, has fixed it so that he will never remember. Yet if he has not had absolutely all his senses knocked out of him and can look about, he will see Kolikongbo a short distance away, on the alert, looking, listening, waiting.

"What do you think of the legend, Bissibingui?"

"Very remarkable, Batouala. But shall I tell you something? To me the stroke of the sun and the legend of Kolikongbo are one and the same."

He laughed softly.

He, too, knew some stories. He even felt like telling one—about the origin of the sleeping-sickness. But it was too long a tale. Some other time.

Djouma growled and snarled. He hurled insults in his dog's language, and made a sudden rush to the border of the path. A few men appeared—N'gapus who had lost their way in the night.

Wonderful luck! Their presence reassured Bissibingui. For that night at least he was safe. He would not be killed that night.

He was sleepy; he'd better profit by this chance respite. He hurriedly gathered up a heap of leaves and stretched himself out to sleep. For one second as he closed his eyes, he thought:

"When I wake up it will be full daylight."

Then his head nodded gently. There was talking beside him. His breathing became even and strong.

He slept.

CHAPTER X

PATHS through the brush, so fresh and dewy in the morning, the aroma of damp earth and damp vegetation, the heavy scent of flowers, quivering blades of grass, murmurings, the rustle of leaves in the breeze A drizzling fog, mists rising from hill and valley up to the pale sun. Smoke, animated sounds: tom-toms, shouts—wake up, wake up!

Ah, there were the birds singing in the trees, and the kites wheeling and wheeling high overhead. And there was the blue of the sky, still higher up, losing its color from the blaze of the sunlight.

What a glorious day! The brush, the whole brush was going to burst into flame. Ey-hey! No time left for you to trumpet, elephants. And you, be'ngues (wart hog) and voungbas (boar), you'd better come

out of your lairs and cease burrowing with
your greedy snouts. Antelopes will be
our prey. Cane-rats will be our prey.
Hedgehogs, too. Roll yourselves into
balls, hedgehogs, let your quills bristle.
The fire won't heed. Buffalos, run, run,
and bellow, run in panic-stricken herds,
plunging, leaping, your tails stretched
horizontal, your bellies to the ground,
swifter than arrows, swifter than the
wind, as if his lordship the lion suddenly
let out his roar.

And you take to flight, too, oualas and
darrambas (hares), you who are afraid of
the very shadows of your long ears, who
trust to nothing but the swift zigzag of
your course. Run, run! Beware of the
fierce tribe of the brethren of Djouma.
No use burrowing in the depths of the
ground brown as your bodies, no use trying your shifts and tricks. Your burrows
are no shelter to you. Run, run straight
ahead, where there's no smoke to indicate
that the brush is burning. Run, run, run!

What a day, what a day! There's bound to be plenty of game. To be sure, there won't be many kolos (giraffes). The great long-legged, long-necked creatures, who can reach the tallest branches, are accustomed to a country that is rich in the prickly plants that they eat. They live in the distant country between Ouahm and Kabo, between Kabo and N'Dele. Ah, the kolos with their tall, spotted bodies!

Nor are bassaragbas (rhinoceros) to be seen any more—those great ungainly creatures with two uneven horns on their muzzles, little red eyes cruel and almost sightless, ugly thick-set necks, and a horrid squeal like a big pig's. Yabao! The bassaragba sees you? Rrou! He makes straight for you—straight for you. Nothing can stop him. Thickets, swamps, trees, lianas. No difference! He breaks, tramples down, rips open, staves in whatever bars his way. Woe to the man who hunts the bassaragba. Woe to him. Woe to the man who strays into the parts

where the great beast first browses, then
ruminates. He'd better beware. He'd better invoke N'Gakoura's most powerful
protection. And should he happen to come
upon the bassaragba's freshly dropped
dung, he'd better be careful not to exclaim
over the size of it; he'd better not say:
"Ouch! How big!" If he does, he's done
for. That will be the last of him. The
bassaragba will come in a fury, snorting
and growling and squealing, his belly dis-
tended and resounding with the perpetual
dondorro of his digestion. In one lunge
he'll knock the man to the ground, then
he'll lie on top of him till he bursts like a
dry reed; after which he'll trample on him,
and keep trampling on him, until his
corpse is mashed into a bloody pulp for
the jackals to share at night. This done—
but not before it's done—he'll trot off,
patala-patala.

What a man should do when he comes
upon a bassaragba's dung is to hold his
nose and snort with disgust and say:

"Ugh, how it stinks!" The disrespectful remark will put the beast to shame, and he'll scamper away as fast as he can.

Kolos and bassaragbas gone—what of it? You hunt whatever there is to hunt. You hunt for the sake of hunting. It is the sport of the strong, the struggle of man against beast; it is skill pitted against brute strength. The chase with its dangers is a preparation for war. Men may prove their skill, courage, strength, endurance. They must have a sure eye, they must be agile, fleet of foot, tireless; they must never pause for rest, or lose their wind, or pant; they must pursue the wounded beast, they must run, run, run, for any length of time.

With the help of the dogs, it is easy enough to catch the smaller game, the hares, cane-rats, and hedgehogs, who dash into the meshes of the wide-stretched bandas (nets) and get themselves snared inextricably. The smaller antelopes may sometimes be trapped the same way. Not so the bozobo antelopes or horse antelopes, the boars, buffalos, and elephants.

Boars and buffalos, unless they fall into the ditches dug for them, must be worn out and driven to bay. But it's when the buffalo is driven to bay that he becomes frightfully dangerous. Feeling death slowly replace the blood that drains away through his wounds, he faces round on his assailants, lowers his head, and charges.

Chatting thus of the hunt, Batouala and Bissibingui walked along together peaceably, Batouala in front, Bissibingui behind, and Djouma coming last with drooping ears.

Every moment added to the numbers of M'bis, N'gapus, and Dacpas who joined them, all armed with javelins, arrows, and throwing knives. The chief wore plumes on his head, and his body was smeared red with castor-oil and powdered cam-wood —for the day of the hunt is a high holiday. Most of the men had dogs with them of the same color and surly temper as Djouma. They marched along singing.

It was fair weather. A soft lazy breeze blew upon the brush from the quarter where the sun rises to the quarter where the sun sets. Lolo still had a long way to go before he reached the middle of the heavens. The tom-toms of the li'nghas merrily climbed the pathless space that rises to the blue villages where Lolo makes his home. The heights of the kaga Biga, which had been crossed and left behind early in the morning, were merged in a mere point on the horizon.

What a delightful day!

The little band of men scattered at the crossing of two paths, the one of which led to the village of Soumana, the other to the N'gapu villages under the rule of Yakidji, the ancient vassal of Snoussi. Each man took up his post for the part assigned him in the hunt, whether watcher, or beater, or firer. The *real* hunters, those who did the killing, were only few in number.

Some of the men went as far as the Dangoua, which unites with the Goutia to flow into the Kilimbi. Here it was that fire would be set to the brush.

Another party stopped before they came to the Dangoua, at the village of the Dacpa-Yera chief Gaoda, on the bank of the Massaouanga. Still others went wherever they chose between the Goubadjia and the Gobo. Batouala and Bissibingui were among these last.

The provisions were unpacked, the garabos, stuffed to the rim with tobacco, were passed around, and the men ate and drank heartily, while Djouma and his brethren made acquaintance in their dirty dog fashion. Then conversation began, the hunters sitting with knees at their chins and heels tucked under their haunches.

"They say," began Batouala, "that lions and panthers hunt in families. Lions do hunt with their mates, that's so. It's also so that while the lioness suckles her cubs, the lion provides all the food. But not for long. As soon as the cubs have sense enough to look out for themselves, father bamara (lion) and mother bamara give them to understand that they would do well to rid them of their presence. Young lions really are fearfully hard to support, like all young people—always wanting more, and still more—never satisfied—their hunger never satisfied. Now if you want something, you must work for it. So father bamara roars 'Douhout . . . dout-dout!' and rolls his terrible eyes, bares his fangs and paces up and down, lashing his flanks with an angry tail.

"There's another story about lions, just as untrue and harder to make people disbelieve—that they roar when they lie in wait for their prey. Nonsense! If people'd stop to think, they wouldn't say such things. See here. If you're on the tracks of an antelope, don't you try to keep as quiet as you possibly can? So why should the lion do differently? If he were to roar, wouldn't that be a warning to the animals he wants to surprise? They'd dart away in a flash. No. Lions roar to express pleasure, after they've caught and mangled their prey. 'Douhout dout-dout! All's well. My hunger is appeased, or soon will be appeased. I am happy. I should like to play hide-and-seek with my shadow in the sunlight. My roaring is going to terrify all the buffalos and antelopes near and far. Douhout! How stupid the beasts are! They've heard my voice all their lives and still don't know that when I roar is the time I'm least to be feared. There! My belly is well-lined. I am strong and I should like some fun. I'll go to the top of yon kaga. Douhout! Ah, how I laugh. From where I am I can see the whole country. And *what* do I see? Far away on the plain I see whole herds of buffalos —running, running, the innocent creatures! because they heard me roar. I must laugh. Douhout . . . dout-dout! **And now I'll go find a cool spot where I can digest my food in peace.'** "

"And how about the people," Bissi-bingui questioned Batouala, "who declare that elephants never rush at human beings but run away at the sound of a musket shot? Don't you think they're as big fools as Kosseyende?"

"I do. And I have a good reason to think so. Several rainy seasons ago I was living at Kemo, and a famous white hunter who went after nothing but elephants was living there at the same time His name was Coquelin. Coquelin was one of the boundjous of whom one sees few. He was as tall as the varas or n'gamas, his eyes were the color of fair weather and shone in his face like the sun in the sky. He wore his hair long, hanging on his neck, and had a long beard. He was so strong that he could fell a buffalo with a blow of his fist. We loved him dearly. He lived as we poor blacks do. He ate our food and slept on a bogbo just like us.

"One morning he was told of a herd of
elephants ravaging the planted fields of
the Gobou villages not far from Ouadda
on the banks of the Ouahmbere where
there are so many alligators. For arms
he took nothing but two rifles, one for
himself and one for his best tracker. The
one he carried was charged with two
shots.

"Chance favored him. Just before sunset of the very day on which he started, he
came upon fresh tracks. He followed
them up, and soon heard a terrible racket.
No doubt now—elephants! There was a
great rushing about, and breaking of
branches, and trumpetings. He could
even hear the growling of their digestion.
They rolled in the mud and sprinkled
themselves with water. For they had
taken refuge from the sun under the trees
beside a lake.

"Coquelin, with his tracker behind him,
crept up, very, very slowly, until he saw

an elephant with his back to a tree. What a pair of tusks! He took aim and—ha! Wounded! In that instant the elephant was upon him. On such occasions a man sees in a flash. If he doesn't die of fright on the spot, a sense of terror doesn't come until afterward, when he has time to think. Coquelin jumped to one side, avoiding the enormous beast, and levelled his rifle again. He pulled the trigger. Bang! A miss! What now? Where was his tracker? Gone, and the other rifle with him. Could he run away? Impossible. Nothing to do but to await death. And death came, surely enough. There it was in those little lively eyes, in the threatening curl of the trunk, in those ears raised and unfurled, in those sharp trumpetings. There it was!

"No one knows exactly what happened after that, because nobody was there to see. But it's generally agreed that the elephant tossed the poor white huntsman in the air; then, to insure himself against further harm, he pierced Coquelin in the belly as he lay on the ground inanimate, and withdrew a few javelin throws away, and died.

"When Coquelin came to his senses, he felt weak, oh, so weak. He dragged himself on all fours down to the river, where he washed his frightful protruding wound. When night came, he wrote marks down on paper, which we learned later from whites meant: 'I shall never see Kemo again.'

"He was wrong. He did see Kemo again. They had found him and carried him back quickly to Kemo.

"He didn't seem to suffer very much, although he was extremely pale, and his body was hot to the touch, and his nostrils were pinched, and his lips were thin and bloodless. Still he really didn't look as though he suffered. And he never complained.

"They hurried up and put him on a mattress and paddled him on a canoe down to Bangui. As it was the season of high waters, they made the dangerous rapids of Bakoundou safely during the night. The doctors at Bangui used all their magic trying to cure him. No use. Nothing could be done. Dondorro had already begun to rot his belly.

"Now the poor white huntsman began to cry. He cried. His swollen belly was like a stuffed wallet. Every night the Mon Pères (priests) watched over him, pronouncing incantations to chase away the evil spirit. In vain. The hand of Kolikongbo lay heavy upon him. He died a week after they had taken him to Bangui."

The sun was at the zenith. Everywhere the glossy starlings proclaimed the news. And from the colorless horizon came the three great gusts of wind that at the same moment daily brought the dirt, dust and leaves flying in a whirl. It blew from the quarter where the sun rises, and died away in the quarter where the sun sets. Today it returned as a faint breeze.

Now, from all sides, from the heights, from the valleys, from the lakes, came the blare of trumpets, oliphants, and tom-toms. Then suddenly a savage yell:

"Iaha!"

The signal, the signal! The chase was on.

Smoke went up from near the Dangoua. Was it really smoke? Yes, yes! Faint, almost imperceptible, at first, it grew denser, blacker, and spread wide in the sky.

The time had come for the clash of javelins on the blades of the throwing knives.

"Iaha!"

CHAPTER XI

AHA! The signal, the signal! The fire on the way, the brutal fire, the fire of many accomplishments. It heats and burns, it starts up the game, destroys the serpents, frightens away the lions and panthers, lays low the pride of trees and bushes, clears and improves the land for the next sowing.

Ah, who shall describe the fire? Who shall find words of praise to express its glow and bounty? Who shall extol this diminished sun which, sometimes singly but oftener in numbers, shines upon the land by day and by night, whether rain or no rain, whether wind or no wind? Who shall sing its lively splendor, its many faces, its progressive warmth, pleasant, insistent, unendurable, mysterious?

Glory to the fire!

When the dustman comes and closes your eyes, the fire purrs and crackles beside you and gently envelopes you with its meshes of warmth; then, as soon as you are completely relaxed in the benevolent little death of sleep, it carries you off to the country of dreams, whence you return in the morning.

If the fever cramps your body and you shiver in a chill, the fire settles the course of the blood that circulates in the blue cords of your arms, it makes you perspire, it massages your stiffened limbs. It is so soft and gentle, it seems like a healing oil. Gradually your muscles turn supple again; fever, fatigue, chill disappear. What though the rain fall outside! There's the fire, inside your hut, to keep the damp out with its glow and to chase the mosquitos away with its smoke.

If you are lonely and sad and want company, no need to seek far. There's the fire again—good friend, good comrade, ouandja, confidant. The fire warms your liver, as it does your limbs, it moves you to intimate confession. To sit beside the fire and talk is a feast of warmth; like every good meal it consoles, soothes, and casts a magic delight.

So who shall praise the fire as it should be praised? Who shall sing its lovely red song when it bursts upon the brush, vast, sudden huge, many-tongued, when it tosses its wild tribe of sparks helter-skelter upon brush and kaga and sends up a confused roar mingled with the crackling of falling trees?

Who shall sing the song of the fire of the brush? It is here and there and everywhere. It is off in the distance already. It never stays in one place. It devours the solitudes in a trice. It leaps from bush to bush. It is coming closer. Patience, soon you'll see it. Wait a moment, just a little bit longer—ah, there, do you hear that furious snarl? It comes from over there where the smoke is rising.

But—but where is it heading? For the

Pongou and the village of Soumana?
Really?

Hey! Poupou (wind)! Poupou, my
good friend, my ouandja, drive the fire in
the other direction. I beseech you, drive
it toward the village of Gaoda. May
N'Gakoura be kind! If not. . . .

Ah, the fire has turned. All's well.
Here it comes. How the smoke gathers!
The air is laden with the fragrance of
scented plants. One last whetting of our
knives and javelins. The time has come!

The tom-tom of the li'nghas. What
do the li'nghas say?

"Buffalos!" the li'nghas say. "Buffalos . . . frightened by the fire . . . galloping toward the village of Nibani."

What else do the li'nghas say?

"In the village of Nibani . . . there
are . . . beaters . . . and firers. . . . The
firers . . . will immediately set light . . .
to the part of the brush . in their
charge."

Iaha! Iaha! Good news—the news of

the li'nghas. Iaha! Smoke goes up from the village of Nibani—black, black smoke.

See the kites! See the smoke! The smoke and the kites hide the sky from view. They veil the sun. Nothing but smoke and kites. The number of kites shows how plentiful the game is. Look! Three of them together dropping straight down to the ground. What are they carrying off? Here's to the chase!

A criss-cross of exclamations, a wild clamor.

Men still kept coming to join the hunt. It was a growing hurly-burly.

The masters and men of all the M'bi villages were there. There were Batouala's head-men, Porro and Ouorro, who stood joking with their mokoundji, and there were the three N'gapu chiefs, Yakidji, Nibani, and Yeretoungou.

Bissibingui was having fun with Kosseyende, the idiot.

Poor Kosseyende! How had he possibly succeeded in dragging himself to the Gobo? He could hardly keep upright on his feet, and that only with the help of a stick. Poor Kosseyende! Koboholo, the sleeping-sickness, had stripped him of his flesh; he looked like a living skeleton. His great bony head dangled from his thin neck, the veins of his neck were knotted into swellings, his hair had turned russet, and his eyes glittered in deep hollows. His limbs, already touched with the icy chill of death, trembled incessantly.

Nevertheless he put his hands to his hips and tried to dance. His knees clicked together. Shouts of laughter went up like a great gust of wind.

He stopped and drew from his wallet two hedgehogs the size of a man's fist. A circle formed about the little huddled creatures. The M'bis and N'gapus present gently clinked their javelins, making a rhythmic jingle of iron on iron, to which, presently, the hedgehogs began to dance, beating time with their muzzles.

Tondorroto (hedgehog), tondorroto,
Ddo, ddo
Tondorroto.

"Ding-ding, cling-cling," went the iron of the javelins. "Ding-ding, cling-cling."

You, hedgehog, you,
Dance, dance,
You hedgehog.

Meanwhile, driven by the full wind, the fire approached the Gobo. No difference to Kosseyende. He laughed a laugh that swelled his throat, he laughed till the tears came.

Ah, the whites knew a good deal, almost everything. But they didn't know that hedgehogs were sensitive to music and that they danced—in their way—as naturally as a dog will swim if you throw him into the water.

Tondorroto, tondorroto,
Ddo, ddo
Tondorroto.

Ding-ding, cling-cling.

Kosseyende's sides nearly split laughing. He laughed and laughed and laughed. Then he began to hiccough. And all of a sudden he collapsed on the grass, his eyes rolling, his mouth foaming.

Tondorroto, tondorroto.

Everybody on the alert now! Do you hear the panting of the fire! It is swelling into a roar. The fire is coming closer, getting hotter and hotter — boiling hot. The smoke is suffocating. Ugh!

Are the ditches for the buffalos well hidden under branches? Yes. Everything's ready, quite ready. To your places, marksmen. Wait now, your eyes keenly intent under frowning brows and your javelins poised in your hands.

A flashing and sparkling and crackling, detonations, cries. Then ashes, bits of herbage, and burnt leaves. Swarms of bees, small birds, and insects of every kind: dung-beetles, butterflies, grasshop-

pers, flies, crickets. Then ashes again—
ashes, and still more ashes.

The wind hastened the onward rush of
the flames. They became visible. Their
long broad tongues licked the herbage
dry and rough with a sound of snapping
and crackling.

A cry. Cane-rats! Another cry.
Antelopes! Cries on cries. Boars, hares!

What a holiday! What sport!

Djouk! Whizz! Two, three, five javelins struck the same beast. The blood
reeked. Ah, the smell of blood! It got
into you like a fever, like a strong drink.

Antelopes! Cane-rats! Porcupines!
Kill the pig-like creatures with long, hard
quills, which roll themselves into balls like
hedgehogs.

Blood, blood everywhere! The chase is
a fierce, red dance. Bah! One rabbit
more.

Look out! Look out! A panther!
Run for your lives. Quick, up that tree!
In that thicket! Hurry, hurry! Where

find shelter? A panther, a panther! Run
for your lives.

Bissibingui had no time to hear or
think. The barking of the dogs, the
shouts of their masters, the glare of the
flames, the heat, the drunkenness born of
the sight of blood and the sight of the
violence to which he and his companions
had abandoned themselves—the tumult
of light and sound and movement had
stunned him.

A heavy javelin whizzed close over his
head.

Who had thrown it?

Batouala.

A moment before, however, Bissibingui,
to escape the panther as it leapt upon
him, had thrown himself flat on the
ground. When he raised himself,
still trembling, the panther had disappeared.

But Batouala was there, very close to
Bissibingui.

The mokoundji lay surrounded by a

group of M'bis and N'gapus. His breath rattled in his throat.

The panther, infuriated by the javelin which he had seen coming—though it was not meant for him—had ripped open Batouala's belly with one blow of his paw. Then he had fled.

CHAPTER XII

THE breath in Batouala's throat rattled faintly.

For fifteen sleeps he had lain like that—stretched on his bogbo, screaming and groaning incessantly, from morning to evening, from evening to morning again. A persistent fever gnawed his bones, and throbbed in his temples, and scorched his body. Every now and then he'd cry:

"Something to drink. . . . Something to drink!"

But he'd throw the drink right up again and fall back on his bogbo gasping with pain.

To-day he was different. No fever, no vomiting, no screaming. He lay bathed in a cold sweat, scarcely stirring, and talked instead of moaning and groaning, talked, talked incessantly, stopping only when the rattle chafed his throat.

A few minutes more, one night maybe, at most a night and a day, and Batouala, the great mokoundji, would be nothing more than a passing traveller. With eyes closed forever, he would leave for that black village from which no road leads back again. He would rejoin his baba and all the elders who had preceded him.

In that village one no longer saw the Pombo or the Bembe, or any of the familiar hills and valleys. The whites were not there to be scorned and obeyed. You couldn't quarrel with this man or that on the subject of women.

Singing and dancing did not last forever. After the dry season came the rainy season. Man lived but a moment.

Here was tangible proof of this truth: here was Batouala. Soon he would die. The calmer delirium following at the end of the day upon such fearful restlessness meant—yes, it meant—the last agony, the lea-lea.

Poor Batouala!

And yet he had received good care. Oh! Not immediately, not right after the accident.

A wounded man was always interesting, especially when his name was Batouala. Agreed. But, for the sake of a wounded man, ought they neglect a herd of buffalos bellowing only a javelin's throw away?

No indeed!

That is why, my Batouala, they left you under the shade of a tree, wrapped in a cover, with Djouma your dog to guard you, while they went off in pursuit of the buffalos. They'd come back and look after you a little later.

N'Gakoura, how tiresome to have to go to the Bembe instead of remaining to gormandize with the rest of the hunters.

Batouala was laid on a litter. Four men with torches headed the march.

Their torches pierced the dark with a smoky light, behind which came the litter-bearers, four M'bis, who were followed by four more men carrying torches.

Bissibingui and Djouma closed the procession.

What a slow step! How heavy! How slow and dull and heavy!

Scents of the night, glow-worms, the rushing of wings, dew, the lingering brush fire dying hard.

And silence!

At intervals, one of the groups of torch-bearers relieved the litter-bearers.

All were equally taciturn. They mustn't walk too fast or too slow, they mustn't stumble or make a sudden movement. At the least jar Batouala squealed like a stuck boar. If N'Gakoura did not hear, that was either because he was polite about it or because he was incurably deaf.

They went along the Goubadjia, crossed the chain of hillocks overhanging the Baidou, and climbed the great bulk of the kaga Biga, the insides of which contained stones of transparent violet which were said by the whites to be precious. When they reached the villages of Debale near which ran the fresh waters of the Kavala, they stopped to rest, eat, and drink, and went on their way again.

A stream, the Bouapata. Farther on, toward Grimari, on the right hand, another stream, the Yakomba. Then, in quick succession, the Yako, its tributary, the Talembe, and a small lake, the last one to be passed, Lake Patakala.

Now came acres planted with millet, maize, sesame, beans, peanuts, gumbos, potatoes, and. . . .

Halt! The hut of the mokoundji.

You are at your hut, Batouala. . . .

The whites had their doctorros, the blacks their sorcerers. Be sure they were alike and one as good as the other.

There were good doctorros and bad

sorcerers. There were good sorcerers and bad doctorros.

But no matter what happened, the orders of the sorcerer must be carried out first.

So, according to the sorcerer's directions, a sort of lattice-work arrangement was set up in front of Batouala's hut consisting of the efficacious fetishes, bags of fragrant herbs, amulets to keep off the evil eye, and bells, large and small, to frighten away the evil spirits.

The evil spirits still lingering, nevertheless, women chanters and players of the gonga came to watch over Batouala.

But alas! it was in vain that they filled his hut with hideous noises of voice and tom-tom. Illness remained supreme. An evil demon tortured Batouala's emaciated body. There was no use any more going to the trouble of tying a rope tight round his belly. Dondorro had overstepped the limits that they had meant the rope to mark for him.

From day to day the gangrene spread. The fat flies, blue, green, and black, that settle on corpses, came and buzzed round the swollen, suppurating wound.

Nothing could overcome the witchcraft of dondorro, neither the clean lavings with hot or cold water, nor the exorcisms, nor the applications of certain cauterizing herbs soaked in spit, nor poultices of cow's dung, nor burning with a red hot iron.

Even Djouma was nauseated by the smell and stopped licking his master's wound. He had fulfilled all his duties as a dog. What more could he do since there was nothing more to be done?

In despair of the cause, the commandant was consulted.

The commandant was friendly and charming. He replied in high humor that Batouala could rot to death and all the M'bis along with him.

So they gave up incantations, exorcisms, amulets, aromatic bags, the sorcer-

er's medicaments, fetishes. The gonga
players departed, and so did the women
chanters. Batouala could die. They had
already begun to pillage his possessions.

Congratulate you, Batouala. You have
not agonized for nothing. Your suffering has reminded a lot of men that you
owed them a lot of things which you had
forgotten about.

They have taken the millet from your
granaries, they have led away your cattle,
they have stolen your arms. But they
stopped short of robbing you of your
women. Rest easy though. The fate of
your women has been decided. They have
been engaged long ahead.

The breath in Batouala's throat rattled faintly.

Of what was he dreaming? Was he
merely dreaming? Did he know that he
was left almost alone in the hut that evening?

No. He was delirious and the breath
rattled in his throat, so he couldn't know

that save for Djouma, Bissingui and Yassiguindja, everybody had deserted him, even his head-men, his kinsmen, his women and the children he had had by them.

He could not know that Bissibingui and Yassiguindja were there separated from one another by the fire that no longer warmed him. He could not know that Djouma, the little yellow cur, was snoring curled up on the rubber baskets—over there. Nor could he hear the commotion caused among his animals by an unwonted sound—the sound of Bissibingui violently drawing Yassiguindja into his arms. The goats capered and the ducks with their necks extended curiously toward the place the noise came from, went pcha-pcha-pcha, pcha-pcha-pcha.

Batouala was in delirium.

And for the last time, in his delirium, he told over all the things he had against the whites—their lying, their cruelty, their illogicality, their hypocrisy. There were neither Bandas nor Mandjias, neither whites nor blacks. There were nothing but men. And all men were brothers. It was wrong to steal and fight with one's neighbor. War and savagery were one and the same thing. But the whites actually compelled the blacks to take part in their savagery—to go kill for them in palavers in far-away lands. And if a black protested, they put a rope round his throat, whipped him with knotted whips, threw him in prison.

March, dirty nigger! March! Die like a dog.

A long silence.

Djouma went to sniff his master.

What was it Djouma sensed? Who had told him that the end was near? Had he wanted to hear from closer by the voice of the man he perhaps mourned in his dark soul? Had the old instinct leapt up in him, which urges animals when one of their number is on the verge of death to forget past quarrels and make truce, and with a worried muzzle separate the herbage and snuff in the direction where, they suppose, lies the undiscernible?

There's no telling. However that may be, Djouma now crouched on the ground as though he were sulking, his snout between his stretched forepaws, his back to the fire.

Yassiguindja and Bissibingui looked at Batouala and shook their heads.

"Is he dead?" she asked.

"Not yet."

They smiled at each other. And they understood each other. Alone in the world, masters of their own fate, nothing and nobody could keep them apart.

Batouala hiccoughed.

Sweet to be alive. Wondrous moment. Bissibingui went to Yassiguindja and drew her into his arms. She yielded to his desire.

Batouala, it is useless for you to persist in struggling against death. Don't you see—they alone exist? They have set you aside. You no longer count for them.

But why have you stopped hiccough-ing?

Ah, your eyes are opening, your eyes have opened, and you, you have thrown the covers off your horribly emaciated body. You have risen.

You walk, tottering and holding out your arms like a baby learning to walk.

Where are you going? To Bissibingui and Yassiguindja? You're jealous, then, up to your very last gasp? Couldn't you let them alone, Batouala, seeing that soon you are to die?

They have no thought of where they are. They don't see you, or, rather, they have not seen you yet. They——

Ah, you've done it! Are you happy now? Are you glad they've separated? Are you glad they're standing glued to the wall, their limbs quaking, their teeth chattering with terror?

And you, ha! N'Gakoura! Overcome by the effort you have made, killed by your own self, you topple over and fall to the ground as falls a tall mighty tree.

The ducks the chickens cackled, the goats ran in all directions. Djouma, from mere habit, growled without opening his eyes. And the white ants never ceased filling their galleries of brown earth to the sound of a long, long steady rummaging. But Yassiguindja and Bissibingui had fled into the night.

Gradually the noises quieted down. The animals fell asleep.

Nothing watches over you now, Batouala, but silence and solitude. The great night has descended upon you. Sleep.

Sleep.